AF447394

Teach Me How To Love Again

Aspen Wolff

Published by Aspen Wolff, 2024.

This is a work of fiction. Similarities to real people, places, or events are entirely coincidental.

TEACH ME HOW TO LOVE AGAIN

First edition. December 19, 2024.

Copyright © 2024 Aspen Wolff.

ISBN: 979-8230603009

Written by Aspen Wolff.

Also by Aspen Wolff

Catch Me if You Can
Obsession
Teach Me How To Love Again

Table of Contents

Trigger Warning!

BDSM themes along with sadomasochism

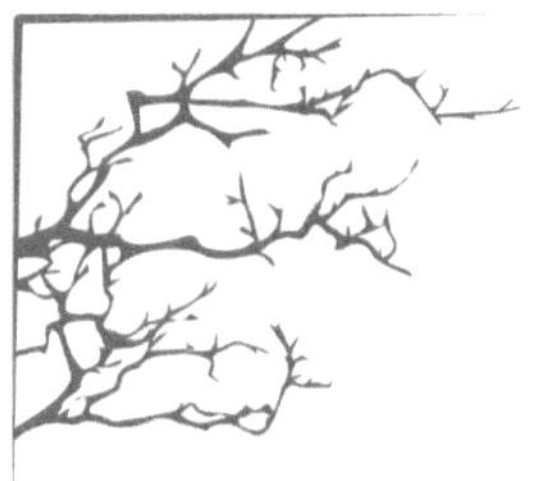

1

Tessa

Five Years Ago

"You can't run forever, baby. I'll always come find you."

I gasped, heart racing as I darted through the woods.

Tingles ran through me, and sweat slid down my temples, making me smile slightly.

I loved it when he chased me... it was so exciting.

I could already feel the heat swelling in my belly.

But, as I ran, I dashed behind a tree and kept going, hoping to throw him off course.

But his footsteps turned, and I glanced behind me to see that expressionless mask glowing in the moonlight.

He was getting closer.

Oh... I almost *wanted* him to catch me. Just to see what he'd do to me.

Almost.

I urged myself forward, laughing for some reason, knowing it would've given off my location, but I couldn't care less.

I was excited, and I wanted him to catch me...

But I also wanted to play.

I wanted to play our game.

But—all the sudden—my foot caught on a branch that stuck out from the ground, and I yelped, falling forward.

I tried to scramble up, but by the time I rolled over, he was right there.

My heart stilled.

And he came at me, making me scream when he shoved me to the ground, burying his face in my neck.

I laughed for some reason, giddy that I could finally feel him this close.

So close I could feel every part of him.

But Miles just shoved me down, making me gasp, and I gazed up at him, eyes glimmering in the darkness.

"I caught you," he taunted, ripping off the mask to expose his face with the light glisten of sweat. "Now... what was your punishment again?"

I thought this over for a moment. "Uhm... take me out for ice cream?"

He sent me a look. "Nice try." He smiled then, making my heart race as the heat down below swelled. "I remember," Miles said then, eyes darkening. "Stay still."

And before I could react, he slid his hand under my leggings, and I cried out, arching my back.

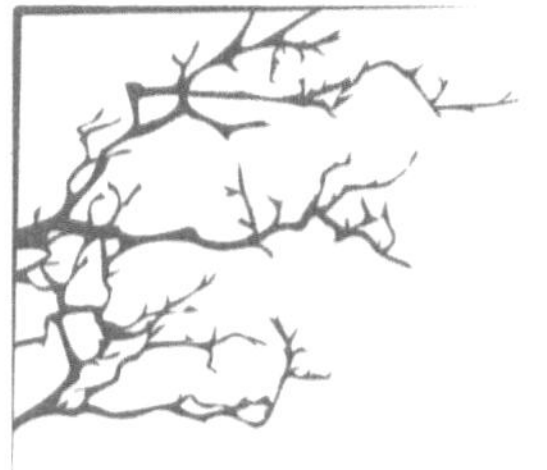

2

Tessa

Present

"Come on!" Alexis yelled, dragging me along the side-walk to Nick's house.

"I told you I don't want to go!" I argued. "Seriously, do you ever listen?"

She glanced back at me. "I'm sure Miles would be so happy to see you."

I glared, heart racing at his name. "Then why hasn't he called all these years?"

She shrugged. "He's been busy. Seriously, babe, chill."

I rolled my eyes as she shoved me up the porch steps and into Nick's house, stumbling as she closed the door behind me.

I turned to look at her, nobody in the party caring enough to give me a glance, and she just gave me her giddy smile before nodding further into the house.

I followed, closing my eyes tightly before opening them again.

She pushed me outside, and I almost tripped, but I caught myself, standing straight up as I gazed across the backyard.

I wonder if he'd be here, honestly. This was Nick's birthday party, and every time I called or texted, Miles said he was busy with his work.

I had a feeling he was pushing me away, so I eventually stopped calling.

"Hey!" a tall, black-haired man called, walking up to us with a girl latching onto his arm. "Alexis!"

I could see her shadow wave from behind me.

I recognized that man from anywhere.

Ace.

He kind of reminded me of Miles in a way, but Miles seemed... *colder*.

"Who's this?" Ace urged, gesturing to me.

"This is Tessa," Alexis explained, "my friend."

The girl next to Ace blinked, confused. "Hold on, what's your last name?"

I was silent for a moment. "Sparks... why?"

She glanced at Ace, and Ace sucked in his lips for a moment.

"What?" I said, taking a step back.

"So, you were Miles's girlfriend?" the girl asked me. "In high school?"

I stammered, caught off guard at the question.

Who was she and how did she know so much about me?

"Yes..." I uttered then, "why?"

"Hmm..." she uttered, staring down at me.

I just took a step back. "I'm going to use the restroom."

I then walked off, rushing inside Nick's house and into the bathroom, shutting the door behind me and pressing my back against it, gasping.

When I closed my eyes to recuperate myself, I breathed out a sigh, hoping to drown out the panic rising inside me.

"You good?" a voice echoed, and I jumped, screaming.

"Whoa—whoa," he uttered, throwing his hands up, "just asking."

I stared at the black-haired boy, eyes widening. "How long have you been here? Seriously? Do you just hide in the shadows or something?"

His long lashes lowered over his amber eyes. "I just needed some peace and quiet. It's nuts out there."

I stared before nodding in agreement.

He then stretched out his arms, letting out a long yawn. "What's your name? You kind of remind me of someone."

I gazed up, confused.

Really? Why?

"Who do I remind you of?" I questioned.

He chuckled low. "That's classified, sweetheart."

I rolled my eyes. "Fine, whatever. My name's Tessa."

He paused then, silent.

I gazed up, finding his amber eyes hardening in fear or anger, I couldn't tell.

"What?" I said, confused.

He got up from the wall and stepped casually over to me, making my breath suck in when his face hovered mere inches from mine.

I watched as his amber eyes searched me, something famil-iar about the look.

I stared up at him. "So... what's your name?"

His eyes locked on mine, and I noticed a smile peak through his lips. "I'll give you a hint," he leaned forward, lips dusting my cheek as he whispered, "starts with M."

My breath caught, and I froze from under him.

"Yeah," he said, chuckling, "now you remember."

Miles.

"I didn't know you'd be here," I whispered, breath shuttering as his gaze raked my skin, burning everywhere he looked. "I haven't seen you in so long... I didn't recognize you."

He stared up at me, running his thumb gently over my lip. "Mm... same."

I closed my eyes as my clit throbbed under my jeans.

Why did I long for his touch so much?

"Miles... stop that." I pulled away.

He watched as I stood a couple inches from him.

"You seriously can't do that," I uttered, shaking my head. "You've blocked me out for four fucking years, and now *this*?"

He just watched me, eyes reflecting amusement in them. "You're hot down there, aren't you?"

I shot up. "*What*?"

He only smiled. "Your breath's shuttering, your face is red, and you're clutching your stomach. Those were your signs in high school, Tessa."

I stared down, eyes widening when I felt myself throbbing under my jeans.

I looked back up to him, cheeks burning.

Goddamn it... his words still affected me like they always did.

He only laughed, shaking his head as if he was disappointed. "All these years later, you're still the same." He stared up at me. "So easy."

Before I could respond, he exited the bathroom, leaving me stranded.

How could he say that? That I was "easy"?

What the fuck was with him?

I shook my head, pulling the hood of my jacket over my dark locks.

I needed to get out of here.

I hated him. He seriously pissed me off.

"**F**ucking Miles," I muttered angrily as I stormed into my apartment. "*So easy*, he says. I'll show him. Mother fucker."

I tossed my wallet and keys onto my bed and flopped down onto it, staring at the ceiling.

God... I hadn't seen him in so long. Why did this hurt?

Why did he look so... *angry* when he saw me at first? *I* wasn't the one who cut him out.

"Mother fucker," I hissed, rolling over onto my side as I opened my dresser drawer, scrambling out a remote.

After powering on the TV, I stayed on my side as the news flashed on.

"*'And we all know that the hurricane is affecting Hawaii, but it is now a tropical sto—'*"

I switched channels, staring at the TV lazily.

"*'Who even are you?'*" a girl on the TV said.

"*'I'm Batma—'*"

I switched channels again.

Knock, knock, knock. "*Penny.*" *Knock, knock, knock.* "*Penny.*"

I switched them again.

"*'And now back to Sharkboy and Lava Gir—'*"

I powered off the TV, sighing as I rolled over onto the other side of my bed.

What did I want to watch? I honestly didn't know.

Maybe a romance or something... like... *Fifty Shades.*

I closed my eyes tightly, an image of Miles flashing by my mind.

But I opened them again, my sight dulling with depression.

I wondered if he hated me now. I wondered if he found someone else.

I was his prize in high school; his possession. We would sneak away on our free hours off school property to kiss and tease each other.

I blinked lazily.

But... at the same time... a lot of high school relationships never lasted. He might've liked me then, but... got into someone else.

I stared at the front door.

He seemed genuinely into me, though... Like... *really* into me in the bathroom.

Why else would he comment on me like that?

Well... he was Miles. He always put on a show in order to suit his twisted desires.

I remembered in our little games; I would always play the submissive.

I covered my face.

Goddamn it, I needed to stop thinking like this.

I slipped off my bed then and headed into the bathroom, rubbing my eyes lazily as I flipped on the light and stepped over to my sink.

I opened my drawer and spread some toothpaste on my toothbrush, and then got to work on cleaning my mouth.

I stared at myself lazily in the mirror as I brushed, finding me looking like a fucking hobo with my hood drawn over my hair, and my clothes stained with white due to the apple cobbler I baked a week ago.

Seriously... I needed to wash this thing.

I looked down to it as I brushed, eyes softening.

This was Miles's jacket. He gave it to me on one of our dates in eleventh grade. We were sitting on a rooftop, watching the city lights, and I shivered, so he put me in this thing.

He told me I could keep it.

I wore it nearly every day; I honestly didn't know why. It was a sense of comfort for me, and due to this, I struggled to wash it every week.

I spit out the toothpaste, rinsing my mouth.

I guessed this jacket reminded me of a younger him; before he put that shield up.

The man who would hold me every night—stroke my hair and... *other* places when we were alone—the man who loved me for who I was and cared for me when my father died.

I pulled my hair into a ponytail, staring at my reflection.

I wondered what happened to him.

I turned out from the bathroom, feeling numb as I crawled into my sheets and flipped off my lamp.

I stared into the darkness for a minute.

I also wondered if I'd see him again.

And I snuggled with my pillow, closing my eyes.

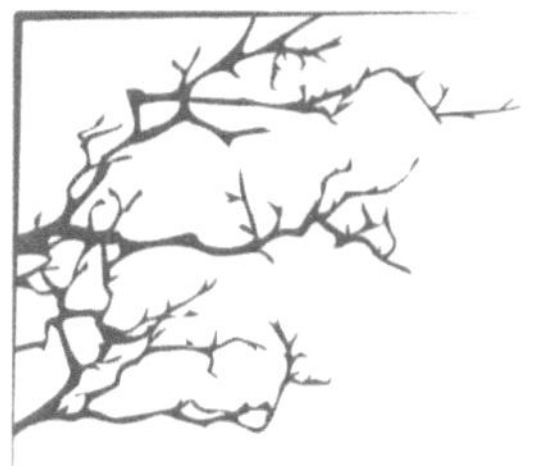

3

Miles

Present

I smiled to myself as I stuck my key into Tessa's doorknob, tossing my hair out from my face when I pried the door open.

They would say this was breaking and entering... but she gave me this key a while ago.

A *long* ass time ago.

On one of her little depression phases because she thought I was ignoring her.

I was, honestly.

But I had my reasons.

Although... she told me that I could come and go as I please.

And I wanted to see her again.

After all these years, she changed:

Her hair was longer, thicker and darker; it reminded me of the night sky. Her eyes were bigger, more emotional, and her body...

Oh, was *that* different.

She was taller, fuller, *curvy.*

It was a complete difference.

She changed herself after all these years. Wow, huh.

Back then... she wore baggy clothes. Now, she wore ones that fit with her curves.

I knew that jacket was mine, but she grew into it; it didn't dwarf her like before.

It actually looked good on her.

I smiled slightly as I locked the door behind me and stepped over to her bed in the darkness.

The covers drifted up and down slightly, telling me she was asleep.

I stopped at the base of her bed.

Wow... she had a *queen*-sized bed? For just *her*?

I narrowed my eyes.

Or was someone else living with her?

I pushed myself forward, anyway.

I pulled back the sheets slightly and slipped in behind her, hearing her moan slightly in response to the movement.

She could slap me, and I'd take it. She could order me to leave, and I would.

I just wanted to see her reaction.

I scooted closer to her and slipped my arms around her stomach, hearing her groan in annoyance.

But I just lightly pecked the skin of her neck, teasing the skin lightly with my tongue as her groans turned into satisfied moans.

She turned slightly, but I kept kissing, lightly stroking her navel with my fingertips.

"Miles..." she moaned softly. "Miles... that's... what are you doing...?"

I stopped then, surprised. "You knew it was me."

She was awake; I could tell.

"I can tell it's you just by feeling you," she replied groggily, making my lips tilt. "Ugh... what do you want...?"

"Seriously?" I said then, arching my brows. "You're not going to call me a creep for sneaking in your house at two in the morning and kissing you while you're sleeping?"

She turned over slightly, sighing into the mattress. "I gave you a key for a reason."

Huh... so she remembered.

"Now will you tell me what you want?" she murmured.

I kept stroking her navel, seeing if she'd react. "I wanted to see you again, is that a crime?"

"I thought you hated me," she replied.

"Hate is a strong word," I responded.

She was silent, and I knew I didn't respond the way she wanted me to.

I don't hate you. Don't ever say that.

"You know..." I said, continuing to kiss her neck as her muscles tensed, and she drew her legs up, moaning, "I'm curious..." I continued.

She turned her head into the mattress as I moved the hand on her navel further... and further down.

"Miles..." she moaned, rubbing her legs together as my fingers slipped under the hem of her shorts. "Miles...."

"Shhh..." I cooed, smirking as I went slower down.

I wanted to tease her; see how far she'd go before she couldn't handle it anymore.

"Miles..." she moaned again, rubbing her legs together faster, "Miles...!"

"Shhh..." I replied again. "The more you plead, the slower I go."

She groaned in annoyance, turning her face into the mattress as I continued, still stroking the nape of her neck with my tongue as she continued to rub her legs together.

When the tip of my finger lightly brushed over her clit, she gasped, tensing.

I only chuckled, going further down with the same pace, hearing her moan as my palm gently brushed against her little button. "Oh…" I said, amusement in my tone, "someone hasn't been touched in a *while*, huh?"

She shook her head, struggling against me as I kept the pace.

I guessed she didn't have a boyfriend then… Just her.

He would've touched her by now; I would've assumed.

"How long has it been since someone touched you?" I wondered curiously as I went further down.

She took gasping breaths, trying to regain her composure.

I slapped her ass harshly, hearing her cry out… and then it trailed off into a moan. "Respond," I demanded.

"I… I… I don't know."

"Sure, you do," I replied. "You have a boyfriend? Do you not?"

"No…" she moaned, still rubbing her legs together. "No…."

"What's with this massive bed, then?" I wondered.

"It was…" she struggled against me still, "my mom's old mattress… She bought a new—Ah!"

I smirked, letting my fingers gently glide down her silky core. "Oh," I said then, "you're very wet. Who knew?"

She turned her face into the mattress, a little more wetness dripping out from her.

I started gently stroking her vulva, and she moaned in response.

"So, very wet," I told her. "Naughty girl. You shouldn't be so aroused right now. You should be pushing me away because you hate me."

"No..." she whispered, turning her face into the mattress. "No... I don't hate yo—*Ah*!"

I inserted a finger into her silkiness, smiling as she tipped her head back, riding my entry as I gently pumped.

"I forgot how good you feel," I told her then, pushing one of my hands down to my throbbing dick.

I started palming myself through my jeans all while quickening the pumps in her pussy.

She let out a sob of pleasure, riding me faster.

I pulled my dick out from my jeans and gritted my teeth, stroking myself up and down while I pounded my fingers inside her.

Tessa cried out, arching her back as her entire body stilled. She came.

I just kept going, feeling my orgasm crest higher... and higher...

Until I hit the edge, burying my face in her neck as the orgasm I gave her still rattled through her body, her walls spasming around my entry as I kept my pace, smiling in her neck as my come still spilled a little on her bed.

After we both calmed, I slid my fingers out, lightly pulling her pants back up over her waist as she gasped softly, easing into the mattress.

"You needed that, huh?" I said.

She nodded slightly.

"Yeah," I replied. "I can tell."

We were both silent for the next couple minutes.

"Well," I said, yawning, "my job here is done. See you later."

She caught my wrist and rolled over, making me look down to her, surprised.

"No," she pleaded softly, "don't leave."

"Huh?" I said.

Tessa's eyes were dulled in exhaustion and satisfaction, but she still scooted closer to me. "You can touch me or whatever you like while I'm sleeping," she told me, "but..." she crawled into my arms, making me blink in surprise as she cuddled into my hold, "don't leave."

"Tessa..." I warned.

"Don't leave..." she whispered.

My lashes lowered, and I sighed, rolling my eyes. "Alright, I won't."

"Welcome to class," my professor kindly said as I walked into the room.

I smiled and nodded, gazing up immediately to find Tessa in one of the upper seats, scrolling through her phone and not paying attention to anything around her.

I smirked.

So easy.

After climbing the steps, I ended at her seat, making her glance up curiously.

Her eyes immediately widened.

I just smirked. "Long time no see." I then winked. "I missed you."

She stared at me for too long. "How did you... get into this class?"

"I'm rich and this is an average college. I got in just fine."

She then looked down at her notes, lips thinning.

"I can still feel your warmth," I said then, staring down at my fingers and rubbing them together. "It's so beautiful, you know. It was so nice and creamy."

Her cheeks shaded over a light red. "Miles."

"Tell me," I said then, gazing down at her, "something about your demeanor makes me curious."

She glanced over nervously, making sure no one was listening before she beckoned me to continue.

"When we were nineteen, we had our first time," I said with a dark smile. "And... then we started getting into other things, don't you remember?"

She looked a little calm right now. "Yes."

"You found out you liked pain," I stated then, making her twiddle her thumbs. "I found out I liked giving it. Are you still a masochist, Tessa?"

She was silent for a moment. "Do we have to talk about this right now?"

"*Answer the question*," I said in my dom tone, low enough so no one could hear.

And no one was listening anyway, it was about fifteen minutes before class started and everyone hadn't arrived yet. Especially the late ones who always sat in the back (where we were).

"Yes," she said then, voice quiet as if she'd never told anyone before.

"Who's your sadist?" I asked her then. "Surely you have at least *someone* who can help you with your desires, right?"

She was silent for a moment. "I... don't have one."

My lips parted. "What?"

"I don't have a partner," she told me gently. "I haven't had... sexual intercourse since I left you. I've been doing it all myself."

My lashes immediately lowered, and I felt a darkness pool inside me. "Was it that hard to get over me?"

"Yes," she said honestly. "To this day I still haven't."

Still the honest little angel like I taught her to be. Back then, when she lied she was punished (with a safe word, of course).

"Tessa, listen to me," I said then, making her lips thin. "I... I didn't mean to hurt you. My father was...."

She gazed over at me curiously.

"My father was taking over the company," I explained to her, "and I left because I didn't want him to hurt you. So I kept you a secret... He checked all my calls and such, which is why I couldn't contact you. I wasn't trying to hurt you; I just didn't want you in danger."

"I know," she responded quietly, "I just wish you contacted me before I randomly met you at the party."

I fell silent. "I thought you moved on."

"I could never move on, Miles," she said then, opening her notebook to a new page as more students flooded in. "You were my sunshine. Despite your dark twistedness, you fucking sadist. I don't think you're truly human."

I glanced over at her in warning. "Excuse me?"

She just smiled slightly, clearly taunting me.

"You're asking for it," I said then.

"I am," she replied.

"Apologize."

"No."

"No?" I echoed then, glare sharpening. "*No*?"

"No."

"You're getting a caning tonight," I growled.

She just kept the smile. "Sounds lovely."

What was scary, is that she clearly meant it.

I smiled slightly. "You're doing this on purpose."

"Clearly."

"You're *asking* for a punishment," I said then. "Where are all your manners? The manners that I taught you all those years ago? Don't you remember? If you talk back, you get a pussy whipping."

She just scratched down the date and her name on the paper.

"Are you going to respond?" I questioned.

She paused mid-word, gripping the pencil tightly.

I just set my hands down. "What's wrong?"

"I... ant... ou..." she whispered.

"Speak louder," I told her.

She was silent.

"My, my. You struggle to get your words out?" I asked her. "I'm going to have to fix that."

She just tucked some hair behind her ear, her face warming with that familiar "I'm aroused" redness.

I just watched her, smile widening a touch. "How about we make a deal, princess?"

She glanced over.

"It's been a while since you've been punished," I told her, making her breaths shake as her face heated further. "Let's make a deal. One night."

Her brows drew together.

"Come to my house," I told her, "tonight. I will show you how it feels to be with me and how beautiful I can make you feel. With the whip marks all over you, screaming and crying... I can only imagine it."

"One night...?" she said then. "A one-night stand?"

"Yes," I responded, eyes dark. "And then... we can move on with our lives."

She just stared at me. "Don't you... have somewhere to be?"

"I have an apartment in walking distance now," I responded.

"Your parents don't like me," she replied.

"My *parents* won't know what happens in my bedroom," I told her, smile widening. "I'm a good fuck, princess. One night with me. That's all I ask."

"Do I have to sign a contract again?" she asked me.

My eyes went dark. "Yes."

She stared at me for way to long, and then smiled. "Fine. One night."

I gazed up at her then, eyes glowing dangerously. "Before that. I think we have an issue."

She glanced over curiously.

"You tested me," I told her, eyes dark. "That needs to be fixed. You are going to come to my house tonight. The front door will be open. You'll find me in my office. You will be there no later than eight, understand?"

Her cheeks glowed a slight red, and she smiled, repeating the same phrase she used all those years ago. "Yes, sir."

My smile darkened.

"**Y**ou're *late*," I hissed when Tessa entered my office. She just closed the door behind her and gazed up. "I've never been here before. I had to find the place."

"I don't want to hear your excuses," I said to her then, and her lips thinned.

I then leaned back in my desk chair. "Now, then. Let's have a small talk before we get started."

She stepped over to the chair in front of my desk and settled down politely, setting her purse aside.

"Do you want to sign a document?" I asked her.

She shook her head.

"No?" I questioned.

She shook her head again.

"Say it aloud, Tessa."

"No," she told me.

I sat up then, setting my elbows on my desk. "Alright. What proofs do you want to see?"

She gazed up curiously.

"It's been a while since you had sex," I told her. "With me. Things have changed. I can show you documents of my STD testing, I can show you reports of my past submissives and how they felt with me."

She shook her head again. "No, I trust you."

My eyes softened then, and I just watched her as my heart warmed.

"Alright," I said then, "you haven't had anyone in a while. Would you like to discuss some things you're not comfortable with?" I asked her. "Degrading names? Flogging? Caning? No condom insertion?"

She just looked up at me. "I'm okay with anything..." her voice grew silent, "just... just don't call me Teresa."

I watched her curiously for a moment, knowing she was stating her full name. "May I ask why?"

She hesitated as if she didn't know how to word it. "Uhm... someone... that hurt me called me that when they were angry."

I narrowed my eyes immediately.

Mother? Ex-boyfriend...? Was she abused?

"Alright..." I said softly, "anything else?"

She shook her head.

"Are you sure you're okay with this?" I asked her gently. "If you feel forced, you don't have to tell me yes, I'll understand."

If she was abused... this wasn't the best idea. It could hurt her... badly.

As if she had a tunnel to my thoughts, she said, "I wasn't abused. I had a small fling a couple years ago with a friend of my mom's, and we got into a lot of arguments. He just refused to call me Tessa, he called me by my real name because my mom did. My mom and I argue a lot, too, we don't agree on anything." She paused. "No abuse, I just associate the name with bad memories."

"Oh, I see," I responded, watching her still. "Alright then. Anything you are okay with directly? Anything you want to see?"

"Oh, uhm..." she thought this over for a moment, "I like vibrators."

"Alright." I noted that in my head. "Anything else?"

She shook her head again.

I set my chin in my hands. "I'm going to go over a small list of things I'm into, okay? You tell me how you feel about them."

"Okay," she said.

"Clit torture," I said to her.

She looked as if she couldn't understand. "Can you elaborate?"

I just watched her stance for anxiousness on the topic. "Flogging, whipping, post-orgasm torture... stuff like that."

"Oh," she said then, "no, that's fine."

"Do you like it?" I asked her, wondering if this would be a better reward or punishment.

"I like coming," she told me. "But uhm... remember when we had sex before, and whenever I angered you, you would slap me there?"

I nodded.

"It's very sensitive," she told me. "It's good for punishment... I guess."

I nodded then. "Alright. What about anal?"

"Uhm... I haven't done it before, but I'm open to try it."

"What about your actual pussy?" I said then. "Insertion. Do you have any issues with that? Would you prefer condoms or skinny ones? Do you have issues with how deep I go?"

"I'm on birth control," she told me.

I nodded then. "Alright, how do you feel about fisting? Fingers? Large vibrators? Massive dildos or textured dildos?"

"Those are all fine."

My, my, she was very open.

"Electricity?" I asked her.

"That's fine."

"Flogging?" I wondered. "Whipping? Caning? Belt-whipping? Bondage? Painful bondage?"

"All fine."

"Sabian?"

"That's okay, too."

I then nodded, watching her fully. "Okay, I think that's it. Now... please, I'd like you to come up with a safe word. Something you'll remember."

She thought this over for a second, then looked at me. "Bubbles."

"You'll remember it?" I asked her.

She nodded.

"Alright, now come up with a non-verbal safe word," I told her. "If you cannot speak or cannot show me your hands, what is your non-verbal safe word?"

She just lifted her hand and snapped three times.

"You'll remember it?" I asked her.

She nodded.

"Alright," I said then. "I'd like you to address me as sir, is that clear?"

"Yes, sir," she said then.

"Good girl," I responded. "Alright. Do you want to see the room we'll be doing these things in?"

She nodded again.

I stood and stepped past her, opening the office door and waiting for her to follow me.

She stood and walked over to me, leaving the room.

"Up the stairs, first door on the right," I told her.

She listened, going up the stairs in front of her, and finally stopped at a specific door.

I opened it for her, revealing an average-looking room with a bed and cabinets surrounding the area.

She glanced at me nervously.

"You can explore," I said to her.

She walked into the room then, looking around before she went to a cabinet.

She opened it, revealing a large rack filled with floggers and canes as well as some vibrators.

Curiously, she went over and opened another cabinet, finding bondage equipment and some minor electricity equipment.

Not afraid in the slightest, she opened every single cabinet she could, exploring the room with an innocent curiosity.

After she was done, she gazed up at me curiously.

I nodded out from the room.

She walked out, and we made our way back to my office.

I sat back into my desk chair and looked up at her. "Now that we're done with the contractual shit, come here."

She stepped over to me immediately.

"Take off the leggings under your skirt," I instructed. "Leave the panties on."

She listened, not afraid in the slightest as she pulled off her leggings and then kicked them aside.

I looked up at her then. "Are you ready for your first punishment?"

She blinked hazily, eyes shading over with lust when she found the sadistic look crossing my face. "What did I do?"

"You tested me in class," I responded, lashes lowering. "That's not something good girl's do."

"What do good girl's do?" she asked me.

I looked up at her then, growing aroused. "After all these years, you don't remember?"

She just blinked. "No."

I glared then. "I told you to address me as 'sir'."

"Why?" she challenged then, eyes glowing with mischief. "I don't have to do *anything*."

"I told you not to test me," I said angrily, glaring at her. "Get over my knee. *Right now*."

The sweet panic grew in her eyes, the lust devouring it immediately.

"I will NOT ask twice," I growled.

"Yes, sir," she said immediately, stepping over and kneeling down.

I caught her arm and threw her over my knee, hearing her gasp in response.

I just set my hand on her ass. "What's your safe word?"

"Bubbles..." she whispered.

"Good girl," I praised. "Are you going to take your punishment?"

"Yes."

I just cracked my hand down on her ass, and she cried out. "Yes, *what*?"

She caught her breath. "Yes, sir."

I lightly rubbed where I hit. "Apologize."

She stared at the ground, silent.

I raised my hand and brought it down onto her ass, a loud crack echoing through the room.

She cried out, back arching.

"*Apologize.*"

She breathed quietly. "I'm sorry, sir."

I spanked her again, and she concealed her cry this time, whimpering.

"Louder," I demanded.

"I'm sorry!" she yelled.

"If you mean it, prove it," I told her. "Get up."

She struggled to stand.

"On your knees," I told her.

She dropped to her knees, her teary eyes gazing up at me.

"Take it out," I said to her, nodding to my jeans. "Prove it."

Her eyes sparkled then, and she gazed down at my pants.

Quietly, she shuffled toward me, settling on her knees fully before she started unzipping my pants.

Gently, she pulled my underwear aside.

My cock sprang free then.

Her eyes widened in amazement, and I watched as she closed her hand around it, starting to gently pull up and down.

I gritted my teeth at her soft skin, pleasure washing through me.

Tessa gazed up at me, silently asking if she was doing okay.

"Mouth, too," I instructed her.

She blinked and gazed down, staring for a moment.

She then leaned down and lightly kissed the length of me, and I grunted, fisting my hand in her hair.

I shoved her head back, and she gasped when I leaned down to her face.

"Mouth all the way on me," I told her in a dark tone. "If you keep teasing me, I'm putting you in a chastity lock, do you hear me?"

She nodded softly, and I let go of her head.

Her mouth opened then, and she just sank it down onto me.

I let out a low growl, tipping my head back as her hot mouth devoured me whole.

She gently sucked, tongue moving gracefully along the head and sending hot tingles through me.

I just spared a look down at her. "All the way down, baby."

She nodded and sank her mouth more, gagging a little, but she continued anyway.

Her eyes watered as she suckled onto me, running her tongue all over me as her soft fingers gently slipped along the base of my cock.

I kept growling, feeling myself grow closer and closer.

I suddenly shot forward and caught the back of her head, fisting her hair in my hands as she whimpered.

I pushed her down further, and she gagged, eyes watering.

"All the way, baby. Keep sucking and I'll reward you."

Her eyes lit up then, and she kept licking me until I reached my limit.

I came into her mouth, holding her head down onto me as she closed her eyes tightly.

I exhaled a low growl. "Drink it."

She succumbed, sucking me harder as her throat moved with her gulps.

I then let her go pulled out of her.

She coughed a little, still on her knees as she caught her breath, some drool slipping from her lips.

"Good girl," I praised, brushing her hair back in place.

A smile found its way onto my face, and I let her regain some composure for about a minute or two.

"Be a good girl and put it back now," I instructed her.

She gazed up, weakened, but crawled over to me, being very gentle and pushing my cock back into my jeans.

I watched her as she zipped it up and then rubbed her eyes, drying the tears from her gagging.

"On my lap," I told her, making her gaze up. "It's time for your reward."

Her eyes lit up again, and she struggled to stand, stepping over to me and getting onto my lap.

I smiled down at her when she straddled me and held her back to keep her from falling.

With my free hand, I opened the desk drawer next to me and pulled out a small egg vibrator, and her eyes widened in fascination.

I caught the remote with my other hand and set it on my desk.

Afterward, I gently lifted her skirt and the pair of panties under it, pulling it to the side and then gently slipping the egg inside her.

She whimpered, closing her eyes tightly.

"Your very wet," I commented. "Do you like that?"

She nodded shyly.

I would've instructed her to speak aloud, but this was her reward, she didn't need to follow orders anymore unless it was in her gain.

I clicked the small little button on the tail of the egg and turned it on until the light flashed (but it didn't buzz without the remote), pulling her underwear back over it.

I picked up the remote from my desk. "Rest your head on my chest."

"Yes, sir..." she responded, shuffling forward and setting her head on my shoulder.

I then wrapped an arm around her back, clicking the remote.

I heard a soft buzzing sound.

Tessa stilled, a soft whimper exhaling from her mouth.

I reached under her and ran my finger along her panties, finding her clit and starting to stroke it in gentle circles.

She clenched, starting to moan.

Instinctually, she rode my fingers, and I just smiled, increasing the vibration with a click.

She tensed, moaning louder as I stroked her faster.

"Do you like your reward?" I teased.

"Yes—yes—yes!" she cried.

"This is what happens when you're a good girl," I told her. "Remember that."

She rode me faster, and then tensed, dropping her head on my chest as she started sobbing in pleasure.

I increased the vibration again, and she started crying softly as I kept stroking her.

"What do you want?" I pressed, leaning down as she kept tensing.

"Can I come...?" she begged, trying to hold it in. "Please, sir? Can I come?"

"Yes," I whispered, "you were a good girl. You can come."

She then exhaled a whimper, shaking heavily as I kept stroking her.

I clicked the remote, setting it to high.

That was the limit.

She cried out, fisting my shirt in her hands when I gazed down at her in amusement.

Her body rattled with her orgasm, and she stiffened heavily as her eyes rolled to the top of her head.

When it settled, I turned the vibe off, and she slumped against me.

"How was that?" I asked her.

"I can't feel my legs..." she whispered.

I chuckled. "You came hard, huh?"

"Yeah..." her tone was lost, blissful.

I just reached under and pulled the egg out from her, and she winced at the action.

Immediately after, I stood and picked her up, letting her wrap her legs around my waist as I carried her to the bathroom.

And now for the kind part of the night, aftercare.

We didn't really do horrific stuff that we had done before, but it was still important.

Gently, I set her onto the toilet, and she hesitantly let go of me.

I knelt in front of her. "Talk to me. How are you feeling?"

She looked entirely confused at the question.

Yeah... I had never done aftercare with her before.

I just smiled. "Does your butt hurt from the slapping? Does your throat hurt?"

She blinked and then nodded.

"Alright," I said then, standing up.

I got some lotion from the counter and some cough medicine, grasping one of my large shirts from the closet, and walked back to her.

She blinked when I knelt down and sighed, gathering the correct measurement of the cough medicine.

I gave it to her then. "It'll help with the sore throat."

She took it and drank it, wincing at the taste before giving it back to me.

I set it aside and started unbuttoning her shirt, helping her out, then followed with her skirt and her panties.

When she was bare, I got onto my knees and patted my lap. "Come here, baby girl. Straddle me."

She listened, grunting softly as she moved to my lap, and she set her head on my shoulder.

I just spread the lotion on my hand and then went down to her ass, starting to spread it along the marks I left.

She relaxed into me at the feeling.

I ran my other hand through her hair, returning to start massaging lotion into her back muscles... and then her neck.

She let out soft sounds at the action, and I smiled down at her.

"You tired?" I asked her.

"Yes, sir..." she whispered.

"No, baby," I said gently. "We're done with sex. You call me Miles now, okay?"

"Okay."

I still ran my fingers through her hair, massaging her back still.

"Alright," I said then, "let's get you in bed."

She struggled to get up, but I just scooped her up and set her on the toilet.

Afterward, I pulled the T-shirt I got over her head and guided her arms through the sleeves, tugging it down to her waist.

"Ready for bed?" I asked her.

"I sleep here?" she responded.

"Of course, you do," I told her, tucking some hair away from her face. "I'll take care of you tonight. That's my job right now."

"Am I sleeping in the sex room?" she wondered.

I shook my head. "No, my bedroom."

Her brows drew together. "Why...?"

"Because you need to be taken care of," I told her, chuckling, "not intimidated by sex toys and floggers."

Her lips parted, forming an "O".

I then guided her arm over my neck, scooping her up seconds later.

"I heard of this..." she whispered, "is this that aftercare thing?"

"Mm—hmm." I opened the door to my room with a shoulder, carrying her in. "The point of it is to ease the mind of the submissive, so she feels safe."

"I like it," she told me shyly.

I just laid her onto the bed, and she dropped onto the mattress.

Her eyes were still hung from her orgasm earlier.

Knowing she needed to sleep soon, I got in beside her. "Do you want to snuggle?"

"Yeah." She nodded.

I laid onto my back, and she shuffled toward me, setting her head on my chest and then finally closing her eyes.

I just pulled the covers more over her and gently stroked her back, lightly kissing her head seconds later.

I struck Tessa's ass harshly with the cane, and she cried out, arching her back as she remained bound stomach-down to the bed.

Her legs were bound open to the corners of the mattress, exposing herself to me, and her arms were tied to the bedframe, as well.

"This is your punishment for being late last night," I said then, stepping around her. "I made it clear that you would not be late."

She just buried her face into the blankets, whimpering. "Yes, sir."

"I don't appreciate it when you test me," I told her, whacking the cane along my hand. "Do you know how upsetting that was? I was waiting for you."

"Yes, sir."

"Why do you test me?" I asked her then.

"I don't know, sir..." she said then.

I lightly set the cane on her back, and she winced. "Why were you late last night?"

"I couldn't find your house, sir..." she told me.

I stepped around her again. "Tell me... were you late on purpose?"

She was silent, and my eyes glowed with their sadistic nature.

I just gritted my teeth and struck her again, and she let out a sob of pleasure, collapsing onto the bed. "Answer the question."

"Yes, sir..." she whispered, whimpering, "I was late on purpose."

I paused and set the cane on my hand again. "Tessa, what is your safe word?"

"Bubbles," she told me.

"Say it when your overwhelmed or it's too much, do you understand?"

"Yes, sir..." she told me.

I wanted to make sure she remembered because she looked on the verge of crying right now. Although, her face was flushed with arousal, I just wanted to make sure she still felt safe.

After I left some beautiful marks, I stepped around her, watching her catch her breath.

I then rose my arm and cracked it down onto her back.

She cried out again, burying her face into the bed.

I just ran my hand along the mark I made, hearing her breath slowly. "You're taking this very well," I said.

"Thank you, sir..." she told me.

"Why were you late?" I demanded then.

"I wanted to test you, sir..." she whispered.

"Did you lie to me, then?" I questioned. "You knew very well where my house was?"

She sniffled. "Yes, sir."

I arched a brow, cracking the cane on her ass again, and she winced.

"Do you understand that lying to me warrants worse punishment?" I questioned.

"Yes, sir..." she told me, smiling a little. "That's why I did it."

I stepped around her and lowered my lashes, immediately raising the cane again.

And I cracked it against her clit.

She screamed, arching her back before collapsing down onto the bed.

I could hear her start crying now, and I just tapped it against her clit again, hearing her gasp.

"You are a bad girl," I told her.

And I slammed it against her clit again, hearing a harsh *clap*! echo through the room as she cried out.

She started gasping when I watched the skin darken to red, and I tapped it again.

"I'm doing it five more times," I told her. "You are going to count each time, am I clear?"

She was gasping. "Yes, sir."

I raised my arm, clapping the cane against her clit again.

She let out a sob of pleasure, her hands gripping onto the bindings on her wrists. "O—one!"

I struck it again, and she buried her face into the sheets. "T—two!"

Again.

"T—t—three!"

I stuck it, once more, hearing her sob.

"F—four!"

And I raised it, clashing it against her clit one last time.

She cried out, burying her face in the sheets. "Five!"

I was satisfied then, immediately stepping around her and going to the cabinet.

She watched me with teary eyes as I set the cane in and then pulled out a vibrator.

Her eyes immediately widened.

I turned toward her and smiled. "You are not allowed to come. If you do, I'll ruin it, and then torture your clit without letting you come again, am I clear?"

She nodded. "Yes, sir."

"You upset me," I told her, stepping around her until I knelt by her exposed pussy, watching the skin redden from my blows. "You are being punished, not rewarded."

She nodded. "Yes, sir."

"I'm holding it onto your clit for twenty seconds," I told her, gazing up. "You are not allowed to come. Hold it in and prove to me you're a good girl. And then I'll think about rewarding you. If you fail, there will be *no* reward waiting, am I clear?"

"Yes, sir."

"Good," I praised, clicking it on.

I then pressed it to her clit.

She cried out, burying her face in the sheets when I held it there.

Her body rattled with pleasure as I held it to her sensitive core (extra sensitive with the blows I gave her), and I raised my hand, looking at my watch.

She started sobbing, tensing her muscles to prevent herself from coming.

"Ten seconds," I told her, watching the second hand swim down the clock.

She gripped the rope tightly, trying her absolute hardest not to come.

"Five seconds."

She tensed, shaking heavily. "I can't! I can't!"

"You can and you will," I told her. "Two seconds."

She tensed even harder.

And I removed it.

She gasped for breath, sobbing into the sheets from her denial.

"Good girl," I praised, lightly running my thumb along her clit, making her tense. "Very good girl."

Tessa pressed her face into the sheets as I stepped back over to the shelf and put the vibrator back.

After I shut the cabinet, I looked back at her to find her staring off into space numbly.

"We're all done," I promised her then, stepping over to undo her bindings. "You did good. Very good."

She winced when she struggled to sit up, and I just helped her, catching her arm and wrapping it around my shoulder.

"I got you," I said, scooping her up.

She moaned in surprise when I carried her over to the bathroom, setting her head on my shoulder.

I closed the door behind me, turning on the shower seconds later and keeping her cradled against me.

Time for aftercare.

And I was going to do better this time because I was harsher with her.

After making sure it was warm enough, I set her down and stripped my clothes, immediately picking her up seconds later.

I then carried her into the water.

She set her head on my shoulder when I helped her onto her feet, and she winced at the soreness from her punishment.

I just ran my fingers through her hair, and she gazed up at me, eyes sparkling.

I moved to grasp some antiseptic wash, and I spilled some on my hands... and then ran it onto the marks where I caned her.

She set her head on my shoulder, enjoying herself.

After making sure her marks were clean, I then moved down and caught some gentler cleaning wash, spreading some onto my hand and then going down to clean her clit.

She whimpered, closing her eyes tightly.

"Sore?" I said.

She shook her head. "Sensitive."

Ah, yes, from the orgasm denial.

I kept cleaning it. "I'll reward you after, I promise."

She sniffled and closed her eyes when I pulled away, and I started washing her hair and scrubbing shampoo into her scalp.

"You're such a sweet girl," I whispered, washing her hair. "A lot of my submissives are afraid of me."

"I'm not afraid of you..." she said then, still snuggled against me. "I said I was okay with anything, right?"

She was different... she was odd.

She was beautiful.

"How are you down there?" I asked her, referring to her clit. "Did I open up wounds?"

She shook her head. "No, sir. It's just sensitive."

"Miles," I reminded her. "Remember?"

"Oh, yes, right." She gazed up, eyes sparkling with her smile. "Miles."

I felt something inside me warm, and I ran my thumb along her cheekbone. "You're such a sweet girl, Tessa. I wish I could spend more than one night with you."

I think she's my favorite submissive.

She was a lot different than she was before.

She just set her head on my chest. "It isn't over yet, right?"

"No," I promised. "It's not morning yet, Angel."

She then snuggled her face into my neck, making my lips part. "Can I wash you?"

I chuckled. "This aftercare is for you, not me."

She looked up with a soft smile. "I just thought I'd ask. You look sad."

I'm not sad. I'm far from it.

I then moved to run conditioner through her hair, and she wrapped her arms around me, trying to hold herself up.

Afterward, I finished, turning off the shower and caught a towel.

I wrapped her in it, and then scooped her up.

She giggled, a soft, innocent, happy sound.

I took care of her then, setting her on the toilet after wrapped a towel around myself.

As I got some pain medicine, some lotion, a hairbrush and toothbrush, as well as *another* one of my T-shirts, I looked back at her.

She was staring at me, in a trance.

I smiled a little when I noticed she was admiring my form with curiosity, and I just finished gathering some things before kneeling down before her.

She blinked, snapping out of her daze.

"You'll reward will be soon, promise," I said to her.

She nodded, eyes sparkling.

I started brushing her hair then, and she closed her eyes, burying her face in the towel as I untangled the strands. After I was finished, I tapped her lip.

She parted her lashes.

"Open your mouth, I'll brush," I said to her.

She listened, parting her lips.

I gently brushed her teeth, being very gentle around the gums as she stared down at me curiously.

After I finished with *that*, I guided her up and held her hair back as she spit into the sink, rinsed her mouth, then spit into the sink again.

I lightly pat her lips dry with the towel she had and scooped her up again.

She giggled at the action, and I carried her over and set her back onto the toilet.

"Take these," I said, holding the pain meds and a glass of water out to her.

She gladly took them and plopped them in her mouth, taking the pills and swallowing them.

I took the cup from her. "Straddle me again."

She listened with no reluctance, dropping onto my lap and setting her head on my shoulder.

"Good girl," I praised as I lowered her towel, spreading some lotion on my hands.

I then rubbed them into the marks left from her caning.

She whimpered from comfort and buried her face in my neck, clutching onto my shoulders.

After finishing with her back, I moved to her butt, and then lightly ran some onto her clit.

She tensed at the action.

"Your reward is next," I promised, once more.

When I finished, I set everything aside and picked her up again.

She wrapped her legs around my waist, keeping her head onto my shoulder.

"Alright, baby girl. Time for your reward," I said to her, and I carried her out from the room.

She held onto me when we passed the sex room and went into my bedroom, and she gazed up curiously when I laid her down onto my bed.

After drawing the covers over her I leaned over, brushing some hair away from her eyes. "Warm enough?"

She nodded.

"Alright," I said then, smiling. "Time to show you how good of a girl you are."

"I don't know what to do..." she told me shyly. "I haven't had sex in a long time other than the punishments you gave me, and the egg. And you used to do everything, so...."

"It's alright," I said, smiling, "I'll teach you."

I then made my way to the end of the bed and sighed, gently lifting the covers to expose her favorite spot.

She raised the blankets, pulling them to her face and gripped them tightly.

I lightly caught her legs and lifted them. "Bend at the knees," I told her, guiding her, "and spread."

She was then open to me, her softness exposing and glistening under the lighting.

I just leaned down... and took her in my mouth.

She moaned, arching her back as she clutched the covers tightly.

"Try to stay as still as you can," I instructed her. "It'll feel better."

"Yes, sir..." she whispered.

"Miles," I corrected, gazing up. "This is about you now, okay?"

She nodded again, clearly not used to this part of sex.

"Say it again," I said gently, "correctly."

"Yes, Miles..." she told me.

I lightly rubbed her clit as she moaned, smiling. "Good girl. And when you come, let me know. You don't have to ask for permission, okay?"

She nodded. "Okay."

I then leaned back down, sucking her clit into my mouth.

She let out a moan, arching her back as she fisted the sheets.

I just suckled the little button, running my tongue along it as she rode me gently.

After about a minute, I slipped a finger inside her, and she groaned, arching her back when I started pumping.

I pulled away, slipping another finger into her. "You taste so good."

"I do?" she sounded shy.

"Yes," I promised.

And I sank my mouth onto her again.

She sobbed in pleasure, threading her fingers through my hair.

When she realized she was holding me there, she paused and then pulled away, grabbing the covers instead.

"It's alright," I told her, gazing up with a smile. "You can hold me there. You can do whatever you want. This is a reward now, okay? Don't be shy."

"I've only done... bdsm," she said, gasping softly as I lightly licked her clit. "I've never... been treated this way."

"You haven't been taught right," I responded, inserting a third finger as she gasped. "And that is my fault. I had to take classes to learn more. The submissive needs feel pleasure, too, sweetheart."

She just tipped her head back, threading her fingers through my hair. "That feels so good... I don't know... how to do this. *Ah*!"

"As I said," I kissed her clit, gazing up at her with a smile, "I'll teach you."

And I gazed down, sucking her back into my mouth.

She moaned, arching her back as I suckled her gently, nibbling her clit, as well.

She attempted to kick out her legs, getting overwhelmed, but I just pulled away, lightly licking it.

"Bend at the knees," I said to her, "try hard to keep them open, okay?"

"Yes, sir...."

"Miles, baby. Miles." I started eating her again.

She just tipped her head back. "I'm getting close...!"

I inserted a fourth finger, and she arched her back, moaning louder.

"Miles!" she sobbed. "I can't hold it in!"

"I told you to come," I said gently, licking her. "You don't need permission. Come when you're ready."

Her back arched higher.

She cried out then, entire body stilling when it hit her.

Her orgasm rattled through her, and I just suckled onto her still, feeling her clit spasming in my mouth when she let out soft, pleasured cries.

It lasted for about twenty seconds, and I kept pumping in and out and eating her at the same pace, hoping to let it last.

When she finished, I pulled away.

She caught her breath then, still shivering from the orgasm as I sat up.

I just caught her legs. "Close," I pulled them together, "and stretch."

I pulled them down, letting her stretch out her sore muscles from all the tensing.

"Good girl," I whispered, pulling the covers back down. "Good girls get rewarded, see?"

She looked very numb right now, and I smiled and crawled over to her.

"Come here," I said then, knowing she still needed aftercare.

I laid down beside her and let her turn into my chest, and I pulled the covers over her shoulders and ran my fingers through her hair.

"It's a while before morning," I told her. "You can rest until then."

She nodded, getting comfy.

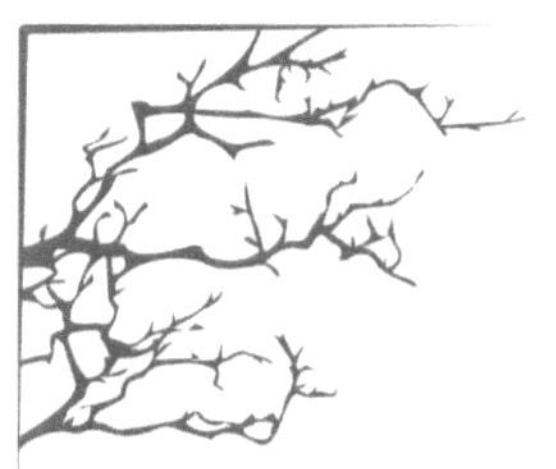

4

Tessa

Present

I t was morning already.

I despised my life the moment I opened my eyes.

Last night was so amazing… I never wanted it to end.

And now that the one-night-stand was over, I found myself shuffling on my shoes in Miles's bedroom, eyes dark as I pulled on my jacket.

He made it clear that he just wanted one night, and then we move on.

It wasn't the best idea to be with him, anyway. He had other submissives… let alone the fact that he was rich as hell, a collage basketball star… and that, well…

He wouldn't be happy knowing that I was with someone else.

After a moment, I clipped my heels on and then stood, gazing up seconds later.

Miles stood in the doorway; eyes dark as he leaned against the wood.

I just watched him numbly.

"Ready to go?" he asked me. "You can stay a little longer if you want."

"No, it's okay," I said gently. "I should be getting home to Alexis."

He scanned me then, as if he sensed something wrong. "Are you alright?"

"Yes," I said then, gazing up, "I just... I cannot stay for long. I only promised you one night."

And I needed to get back to my apartment ASAP in case *he* came back.

Miles just stepped over to me, eyes dark.

I just gazed up at him, and he stopped in front of me.

He tipped my head up gently, making me closed my eyes when his breath dusted my cheeks. "Stay."

He set his lips on mine... and this kiss wasn't anything like before. It was needy, desire-filled, desperate. There was no lust, no playing in it... no teasing.

Something hollow filled me, and I pulled away. "Bubbles."

I regretted it the moment it came from my mouth, and I closed my eyes tightly when the hollow feeling deepened.

Miles immediately separated from me, taking five steps back to give me distance.

His eyes were darker than I had ever seen them, and I just breathed shakily, catching my purse.

He remained silent, looking slightly pained as if he feared he screwed up.

But it wasn't him that did, it was me... but there was nothing I could do now.

I had to keep myself and Alexis safe.

"I have to go..." I said gently.

He avoided eye contact, instead focusing on the floor. "I'll walk you to the door."

I could tell by the look in his eyes that he didn't want me to go, that he was resisting the urge to beg me to stay.

But he respected my safe word and kept a distance, not pressing me any further.

I stepped past him and into the hall, and he followed behind me.

Once we entered the main level, my phone came to life in my pocket.

My lips parted, and I stopped, pulling it out.

It was Alexis.

I immediately answered and pressed the phone to my ear. "H—hello?"

"Tessa…?" she whispered quietly. "Where are you?"

"I'm uh…" I glanced at Miles nervously to find his eyes on my, but I stared back forward, "at a friend's house. What's up?"

Alexis's voice shivered, and my eyes darkened.

"*Alexis,*" I pressed, tone sharpening. "What's wrong?"

She just breathed quietly. "Sorry. I'm just not able to focus right now."

I immediately questioned her, "Did he come back?"

Miles was focused on me now, getting suspicious, but I ignored him.

"*Alexis,*" I said.

"Yes."

"I'm coming," I demanded, starting to the front door.

"Tessa, no!" she yelled, making me pause. "He's out there somewhere! Stay at your friend's house for a little longer! You know he wants you, too!"

"I don't care that he wants me, too," I demanded, starting to Miles's office to grasp the last of my belongings. "I'm not afraid of him. I'm coming."

"Tessa," Miles said, "what are you talking about?"

I ignored him, hyper-focused on Alexis right now and making sure she was okay. "Did he hurt you?"

"No... I slammed the door in his face."

"Did you call the police?"

"Yes, they're on the way."

I swung my purse over my shoulder. "I won't let him hurt you, Lexie. Hold tight."

"If anything *you're* the one who should be afraid!" Alexis cried. "You're the one he's hunting, Tessa! Just stay there! The police will be here soon! I don't want you chasing after me! You're going to get yourself killed!"

"I don't care if I get myself killed," I stated. "I won't let him hurt my friends. Now I'm coming. Call me if he knocks again." And I hung up.

Before I could grasp the doorknob, Miles caught my shoulder.

I glanced back at him, irises beating in fear.

He just caught his keys from the hook beside the front door. "I'm driving you."

"No," I said sharply, "you stay here."

"You can't protect everyone, Tessa," he told me, making my eyes widen. He just smiled. "The volume was loud. I could hear her."

I just gritted my teeth and started to the front door. "You're staying here, and that's final. I can take care of this. I don't need your help."

He caught my wrist, hard enough to make me wince.

I glanced over at him in question.

"I'm the boss around here," he told me in a dark tone. "You are in my house, therefore, you are my submissive, are we clear?"

"Miles..." I whispered.

"Tessa, you're putting yourself in danger. Let me at least go with you, so you're not alone."

"Why do you care?" I snapped then but immediately hesitated. "You can't... you *shouldn't.*"

"Why?"

"If he knows I spent the night here..." I trailed off.

If he found out, he'd kill Miles. And that wasn't an exaggeration. He had killed before.

The police had been searching for him for ages... they could never find him, but he kept finding me even when the police were outside my house.

I just looked up at Miles. "Let go."

"Either I'm going with you," he said, holding me tighter as he glared, "or you're staying."

I just gritted my teeth. "Bubbles."

He released my arm, but stepped in front of the door, blocking it. "I won't touch you then, but I'm still enforcing it."

I just glared sharply. "Get out of the way."

He crossed his arms across his chest. "No."

"Miles... don't do this," I whispered.

"Those are my two options," was his response. "You're lucky I'm giving you an option. If you'd like to argue with me more, I'd be happy just to force you to stay."

I closed my eyes tightly. "Miles."

"Ten seconds to decide," he responded in a dark tone.

I gazed up then. "You're not the police."

"I'm a trained athlete," was his response, referring to his basketball job. "And trained in the army. Five seconds."

I just gazed up. "I'm sorry."

His brows drew together.

I immediately shot up and stuck him across the face.

He cried out, falling sideways and collapsing onto the ground.

Immediately, I shoved open the front door and ran out, starting my car and then speeding off.

Oh, God—oh, God—oh, God. He was going to be pissed. He was going to be really, really pissed.

I was in for it now.

But I kept driving, knowing it was better to be punished than possibly losing someone else close to me.

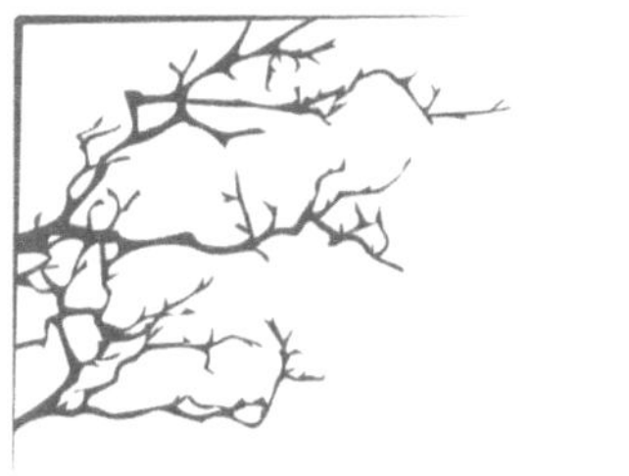

5

Miles
Present

That fucking bitch.

I gripped the steering wheel tightly as I followed after Tessa's car, the blow on my cheek still throbbing angrily.

I after she hit me and ran off, I was able to rush after her and get into my car before she left my street.

I needed to know what was happening. What would make her hit me like that? She had never gone that far before.

Everything I heard... someone wanted to hurt her? Someone attacked Alexis?

What the fuck was happening?

After a moment of ruminating, I pulled out my phone and dialed my friend, Ace.

It rang for like two seconds before he picked up.

"Yo! Miles! Sup?"

"What do you know about Tessa?" I demanded angrily.

He just sighed. "What did she do?"

"Answer."

"Damn, for you to be this mad, she did something *bad*," Ace said then, sighing. "Well, uhm... I know her and Alexis are close. They're roomies. And I know that Tessa and her roomed up about a year ago. Tessa's been very distant, though. You know that Alexis has been around us almost every day, Tessa outwardly refused to come with. Alexis had to force her to come to the party. She told me she had to drag Tessa out the door. I guess Tess's been avoiding us."

My brows drew together. "Why?"

"I don't know," Ace responded. "I assumed it was because you and her had some patchy places, but... I don't know if that's true."

"Has Alexis mentioned anything about a guy following her around?" I questioned.

"Yeah," Ace responded. "She said there's a creep stalking her. She's been spending night's at Kylo's lately."

Yeah... her and Kylo were *oddly* close despite her being a prostitute.

"Wait..." I paused, "does that mean that Tessa's been alone?"

"Yeah," Ace said then. "But she seems to want it to be that way, so who cares?"

I just gritted my teeth at his coldness. "Alright, bye."

"Wha—"

I hung up immediately and dialed Kylo.

It rang once, then twice.

He picked up. "Damn. It's been a while since you called me, bro."

"What's going on with this guy that's been stalking Alexis and Tessa?" I questioned him.

"Well, hello to you, too."

"Answer the question."

He just sighed. "Alexis said there's some creep who's been around her apartment lately. She refuses to talk about it, claiming that it's better if I don't know because I'll get violent."

"Yeah, you have violent tendencies," I responded.

"Says the sadist."

Yeah, out of all my friends, Kylo was the only one who knew that I was secretly a sadist and that I had submissives in my house a lot.

"Shush," I responded, "is this guy dangerous?"

"Enough for Lexi to come to my house and give me blows for free so she can stay the night?" Kylo responded. "I'd say, yes."

I just sighed and gritted my teeth.

Just who is this guy?

"Have you seen Tessa lately by chance?" I questioned.

"A couple times, yeah."

"Has she mentioned anything about this guy? His name? How dangerous he's been?"

"Nope. Lips sealed shut. Alexis does most of the talking... and she's been giving me bullshit."

Something told me Tessa wasn't being silent due to stubbornness, something told me she was afraid of him.

"Alright," I responded, "where is Tessa and Alexis's apartment?"

"Uh..." he said then, "800 South Kell's, I think?"

"Thanks," I responded. "By—"

"Hold up before you hang," he said, tone sharp. "You have your angry tone, and not the 'I wanna whip a girl' tone, you have that protective tone. Did something happen?"

I was silent for too long. "How much do you care about Alexis?"

He was silent for a moment, but his tone shifted to something dark. "Why?"

"How much?" I said then. "Do you care? If you're just there for blows and giggles, then I'll drop it."

He silenced for too long. "The fucker came by again, didn't he?"

"Yup," was my response.

"I'm going to fuck him up," Kylo growled, immediately standing from where he was sitting.

"I guess I'll see you there?" I smirked, knowing that his "relationship" with Alexis was more than he let on.

"Shut the fuck up," he hissed.

And he hung up.

Knowing the fact that he immediately got protective was a sign that this guy was nothing to mess with.

I was glad I followed Tessa, or I'm sure this wouldn't have ended well.

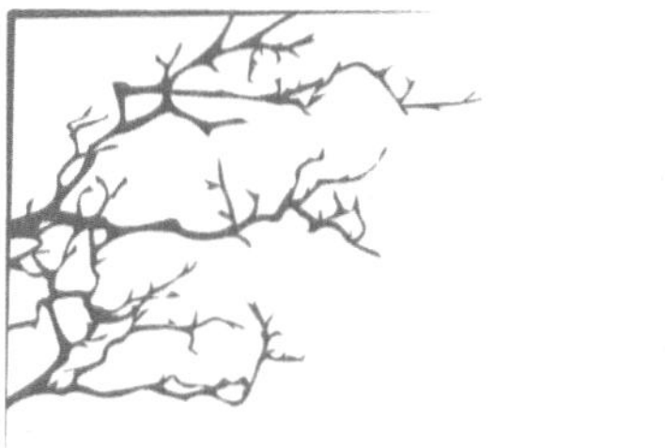

6

Tessa

Present

"Shhhhhh…" I soothed, rubbing my hand on Alexis's back as she rocked herself on the floor of her bedroom. "It's alright."

"No, it's not…" she whispered, "he's going to kill us."

I kept rubbing her back. "Why don't you stay with Kylo for a little? You feel safe with him, no?"

She just stopped rocking and shuffled toward me, pulling me into a hug when I stilled. "I can't leave you like that…" she said quietly, "I can't leave you to him like that."

"Alexis… I've been handling him for years," I told her. "It was *me* who brought you into this mess. Please… just go with Kylo."

She just sat up, glaring angrily. "You're an *idiot*!"

"Alexis," I said gently, "I can handle him myself."

She immediately slapped me across the face, and I grunted, the pain bursting through me.

"You *dumbass*! You're going to get yourself KILLED, you IDIOT! HOW DARE YOU TREAT YOURSELF LIKE THIS?!" She raised her hand to hit me again, and I winced, preparing for it.

"That's enough," someone said from behind me.

57

We both stilled, gazing over.

And found Miles standing at the door, arms crossed over his chest.

My eyes widened in horror, and I started breathing shallowly as I struggled to keep myself sane.

No. No. No.

HE FOLLOWED ME?!

THE IDIOT!

The front door just closed behind him, and I heard a soft voice: "Lexie?"

Alexis immediately stood, eyes widening. "Kylo?"

Immediately, she ran past Miles to greet him, leaving me and Miles alone.

I stared down at the ground, breathing shallow as I tried to calm myself.

Miles just stepped around me and sighed, settling on the floor beside me.

"Look at me," he said gently.

I hesitantly gazed up.

He lightly tipped my chin to the side and ran his thumb along my cheek.

I winced when a soft burn spread through my skin.

"She hit you hard," he commented, pulling away.

I remained silent, avoiding eye contact.

He just watched me, setting his arms on his knees. "You're afraid, aren't you?"

I shook my head quickly.

"Don't lie to me," he said then, eyes darkening. "You know how I don't like being lied to, Tessa."

"Tessa," Alexis said from the doorway, making me quiet more, "if you don't tell him, *I will*!"

Kylo stood next to her, a hand around her waist as he danced his fingers along her hip.

"Alexis," I whispered, still feeling the blow from her hand.

"His name is Johnathan Micheals," Alexis explained, making me close my eyes tightly. "He's Tessa's ex-boyfriend."

"What?" Miles said then, immediately looking down at me.

I remained silent.

"He's a fuckwad," Alexis snapped then, making Miles gaze up curiously. "He started as a fling with Tessa, but her fuckass father sold her to him."

"SOLD HER?" Miles echoed.

"Her father's a dick," Alexis snapped, clearly enraged right now, and I couldn't blame her. "He sold Tessa to fuckwad Johnathan to marry in return for a fucking business."

Miles stared down at me then, but I remained silent.

"Fuckwad didn't marry her," Alexis said then, "fucking kidnapped her and held her hostage, wouldn't let her leave. Fuckwad turned out to be a fucking serial killer known as Jack the Reaper. That's what he called himself. Held her hostage and locked her in a room, gave her food and water in return that she'd cook and feed him. Didn't touch her, abuse her, fuck her. Just used her as a fucking slave."

Miles just leaned down to see my face, but I just hid it more. "Is this true?"

"Tessa's lucky-ass escaped," Alexis said then, gritting her teeth. "Pissed him off because he's an asshole. Now fuckwad wants to kill her. He's been hunting her for years. Thinks she's his *plaything*. Police have been searching for his sorry ass but can't find him because little miss idiot here refuses to talk to them."

Tears filled my eyes, and I hid my face.

I didn't blame her, honestly. John hadn't shown himself for ages, so I thought I could room with her. But he wasn't done hunting me... once I roomed with her, he started targeting her and me both.

I understood that she blamed me.

I felt my tears slip down my chin and drop onto the ground, and I started shaking.

"Are you done being an idiot, Tessa?!" Alexis snapped. "*Talk to the fucking police before he kills us all*! DO YOU WANT OUR DEATH ON YOUR HANDS?"

"Enough," Miles cut in, shooting her a look. "She's already crying, stop."

Alexis silenced then, and I felt Miles's eyes on me as I cried softly.

"Why won't you talk to the police...?" Miles asked me gently.

"He'll kill them," I whispered somberly, "he'll kill you; he'll kill all of you. He'll kill everything... it's all my fault."

"Lexie, let's go," Kylo cut in then. "Leave the sorry bitch to cry."

His words cut me, and I sank in on myself, the cold burrowing deeper into me.

"Shut the fuck up!" Miles growled then, looking up at his friend. "You do not talk to her like that, understand?!"

He just scoffed. "All this is her mess! She didn't have to bring Lexie into this! Let's go Alexis, now."

He walked off.

Alexis didn't say anything then, just stood there for a moment before she left with him.

Miles stayed with me, though, his eyes completely dark as he watched me.

He looked like he was simmering inside, wanting to go over and strangle Kylo until his brain exploded, but he stayed with me for some reason.

"He's going to kill you now..." I whispered to him.

"Not if I kill him first," Miles responded darkly. "Sorry... give me one second, okay?"

I nodded, knowing he probably needed space.

He just stood, pulling out his phone and dialed someone.

It rang once, twice, three times.

And picked up.

"Hello?" Ace's voice was silent, but the volume was loud enough to register what he said.

"Ace," Miles said, "call your bodyguards to protect Aspen and you. All of us are in danger."

"What?" he responded.

"Treat it like an Orion and Christian situation," Miles said then, and I knew he was referring to the situation with Aspen's attempted murder. "He's after Tessa."

"Shit," Ace said as if he was used to this kind of thing, "you need me to hire some for you, too?"

"No," Miles said calmly, "I have some of my own."

I gazed up hazily.

Bodyguards...?

Miles had *bodyguards*?

"Aight," Ace said then. "Thanks, bro."

"Welcome, oh, and," Miles tone darkened, "beat the fuck of out Kylo for me, would you? He's made Tessa cry."

"Will do," Ace said then, "still need to fuck him up after what he did to Aspen."

"Alright," Miles said then, "ta-ta."

"Bye."

He hung up and dialed someone else.

"Yo—yo—yo," Nick said then.

"Hire bodyguards for yourself, please," Miles said then. "Unless you want to die."

"Lemme guess..." he said, "another Orion and Christian sitch?"

Were they just used to this kind of thing...?

"Basically."

"Kay," he responded casually. "Thanks, bro."

"Peace," Miles said, hanging up.

He then sighed and dialed someone else, gazing down at me briefly to find my curious expression.

The people picked up.

"Hey," Miles said then, "I have a Code 120. I need protection for me and someone else from Johnathan Micheals? Also known as Jack the Reaper."

"Ah, yes the infamous Jack the Reaper." She sounded calmer than I had ever heard someone when saying his name. "Code 120? Alright, we found your location, we're sending five men to you and... who is the other someone?"

"Tessa Sparks," Miles said then. "Age twenty-three. Height five-foot four. Social ends with four-twenty-two-oh."

My mouth dropped open.

Don't just give them my information like that!

"We have her information," they responded immediately, making my eyes widen. "Thank you, they'll be there soon."

And the phoneline clicked.

Miles gazed down at me.

"I'm... what...?" I said then.

He just smirked. "Ace, Nick, and I are very wealthy and famous people. People try to kill us all the time. We grew incredibly paranoid when Aspen was targeted and almost murdered, so we have a service we found full of retired assassins who are trained to protect us when we're in danger. They won't stop until he's dead, Tess."

I couldn't breathe. This all seemed too unreal.

"I'll make sure to give your father a call," Miles said then, sighing as he glanced down at his watch. "Oh, look. It's almost time for dinner. Let's go."

"I'm..." I was silent for a moment, "I'm going with you?"

He looked down at me again, eyes dark. "If you want. I can give you space if you want, too. They're going to be here soon, anyway. He can't hurt you anymore." He was silent for a moment and knelt by me. "I'm sorry if I scared you too much. Enough for you to say your safe word twice. I can leave you alone for a little if you want, Tessa."

I just watched him for a moment, then hesitated. "Uhm...."

"Hmm?" he said then.

"I said the safe word because I was scared," I explained to him nervously, "I was scared that if he found me with you, he would target you immediately, but...."

"So... so last night wasn't too much?" Miles asked me.

I shook my head quickly. "No!" I flushed at the words before I quieted. "No, it wasn't. I loved every second. I was just scared, that's all."

A smile formed its way onto his face, and he just sat fully. "I have a guest bedroom. You can stay there for a while until all this passes. Unless..." he was silent for a moment, "you want to be here instead."

"I don't want to be alone," I whispered. "Especially now that..." my heart cracked at Alexis's words, "that she hates me. But..." I sighed shakily, "just... just take it slow with me, okay? I've been distant a lot... I'm not very... *social*. I speak with my body mostly with you, anyways, but still."

I felt my cheeks heat despite the hollow feeling.

I knew how to use my body to express my desires... especially my twisted ones. I loved pain and I loved satisfying the dominant (Miles) all those years ago. But I'd never really felt attached emotionally... especially with how long I'd been distant with Miles.

All those years cooped up with John... I forgot how it felt to love. I lost my will to freedom a couple times, but... with Alexis, she tried desperately to get me to socialize, but I didn't know how.

Especially with my dad and how much he hated me... hated me enough to sell me off for money. And how I thought the one I was supposed to marry was going to be kind, but in reality, he betrayed me.

I forgot how to love. I don't know if I ever knew how to love.

Miles smiled then, gently. "Alright, we'll take it slow, then."

I watched his kind smile... and I felt something deep inside me burn.

I had a secret desire that maybe... maybe Miles... could help me learn my desires again, guide me to find the ways I liked to be touched, he could train me to ask for what I wanted, he could make me feel good again. Like he did when we were so young...

Maybe he could teach me how to love again.

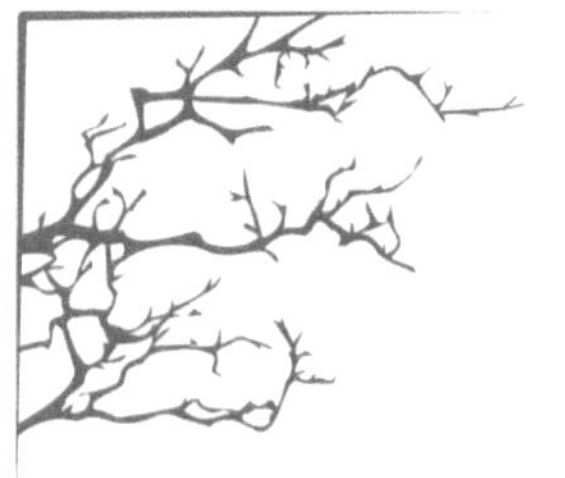

7

Miles

Present

"Is that the last of your stuff?" I asked Tessa, setting one last suitcase onto the floor of the guest bedroom.

She looked at me and nodded.

After the bodyguards came, she and I packed all of the stuff from her apartment into some trash bags and suitcases, lastly bringing them here.

It was a last-minute hurrying moving tactic she learned a while ago, is what she told me.

I smiled. "Alright. Well, I'll let you settle in."

"Miles," she said before I could leave.

I paused, looking back at her. "Hmm?"

She looked oddly shy and embarrassed right now. "Thank you. For letting me stay."

I just watched her stance. "There's no need to thank me, Tessa. Now get settled in."

She nodded. "Yes, sir."

I just left the room, making my way to mine in order to get things of mine settled.

It was an hour later—about nine o'clock at night—and I found myself in my bedroom, sitting on my mattress while typing on my phone.

A low knock fell on my door.

"Come in," I said.

The door creaked open, and I looked up to find Tessa standing there with an indecipherable expression on her face.

She stood there, watching me.

"You can come in," I told her again, setting my phone aside. "Is there something you needed?"

She stepped in the room and closed the door behind her.

Almost immediately, she started pulling off her shirt.

I stilled, eyes widening.

"Tessa, what are you doing?" I demanded harshly.

She knew better than to strip uninstructed like this.

After, she tugged off her skirt and unclipped her bra, lowering her panties and kicking them aside.

I glared, not liking her testing me.

When she was bare to me, she immediately got onto her knees.

My anger immediately erased, and my brows drew together.

She lowered her head submissively, her hair falling over her shoulders. "I hit you earlier today," she told me gently. "I'm sorry, sir. You can punish me if you'd like. I'll take it willingly, sir."

My lips immediately thinned, and my lashes lowered. "Tessa."

"I deserve it," she said to me. "Punish me, sir. Do whatever you like... you can spank me, cane me, flog me. You don't have to reward me this time. Anything you want."

I immediately stood and stepped over to her, kneeling down. "Look at me."

She gazed up, her eyes glistening sadly.

I just watched her expression for a moment.

"I can suck you again," she told me desperately. "I'll take whatever punishment you want."

I just sighed. "Get up."

"Yes, sir…" she whispered, struggling to stand.

I stood with her, and she just kept her head lowered submissively.

"Put your clothes back on," I said to her then.

She gazed up, brows drawing together. "What…?"

"You heard me," I replied.

"I hurt you…" she argued. "I made you angry. Aren't you going to punish me?"

"Clothes on," I demanded. "I won't ask again."

She listened then, stepping over to her undergarments and slipped them on, finishing with her T-shirt and skirt.

She then looked up at me, her eyes glistening with a question:

What do I do now?

I nodded to the bed. "Sit."

"Yes, sir." She stepped over to the mattress and settled down onto it, gazing up at me seconds later. "What do I do now?"

"Tessa," I told her then, eyes dark, "I not going to punish you for that."

Her brows drew together. "Why…? Is it because I asked for it…?"

"You didn't ask for it," I corrected. "You feel guilty for hitting me, so you want me to hurt you to make me feel better. That's not how this works."

Her brows draw together. "It's not…?"

"Tessa," I said gently, "the punishments are for your sexual pleasure and mine. If I punish you because I'm mad and you aren't getting pleasure from it, that's not good. That's physical abuse."

She seemed taken aback at my comment, and then her face paled. "I'm not accusing you of anything!"

"I know," I said gently, "it's alright."

She settled back into herself, looking shy now. "Is it because... you don't want me?"

"Sweetheart, punishing you for trying to save me goes against my morals," I said to her, making her brows draw together. "Before you hit me, you apologized, remember?"

She nodded. "Yes, sir."

"Let me make myself clear," I told her, eyes darkening. "You are to *not* ask for punishments if you only want to please me, do you understand?"

Her eyes widened at the anger in my tone.

"I might be a sadist," I said to her, tone softening, "but I do not get pleasure from just hurting you. I get pleasure from you *enjoying* it. Does that make sense?"

She stared for a moment before she nodded.

"Alright," I said to her, "now... what do you want for dinner?"

"Miles..." she whispered.

I looked over at her, brow arching.

"I don't..." she hesitated, breaths straining.

"Yes?" I prompted. "Finish your sentences, Tessa."

She pushed forward then. "I was gone for so long. I've been kept from you for so long, from *people* for so long. And I don't blame John. It's me, too. I've been keeping myself from people in order to keep them safe." She was silent for a moment. "I'm sorry. I don't really understand how to talk to people or how to... how this works, you know?" Her voice grew quiet, and I could barely hear her. "I forgot... how to love."

My eyes immediately softened, and I just stepped over to her.

She avoided eye contact, looking very uncomfortable.

I knelt to her level, so I could see her face. "Do you like me, Tessa?"

"Yes..." she said gently.

I just raised my hand, running my thumb along her cheek as she gazed up. "Then I can teach you."

Her brows drew together. "Teach me...?"

"I can teach you how to love again," I told her.

Her cheeks burned a bright red, and her eyes widened in confusion.

"We can explore," I said to her, smiling, "all your desires. You like to feel pain, we can check that off the list. You like vibrators, we can check that off, right? But there's a lot more to explore, don't you think? I can help. I can help you find yourself. What makes you scream, what makes you beg... your most favorite things. Do you like the sound of that?"

She nodded quickly.

"Good," I said then, "but tonight... not tonight. Maybe tomorrow or the day after. Because tonight, you need to rest. Especially after what happened with Alexis and fuckwad serial killer. You look..." I scanned her, "a little too damaged for punishments tonight."

"Is that..." she hesitated, "a bad thing?"

"No," I assured her. "It just means you need a break."

Her lips parted.

I smiled then. "And what better break than to order in some Chinese food, huh?"

A small smile formed on her lips. "That sounds nice."

It was late that night, and I was half-asleep when I heard my door creak.

I parted my lashes, gazing up briefly to see what opened it.

A small, frail figure stepped in the room, glancing around before looking down at me.

Thinking I was asleep, she closed the door behind her and stepped over to my armchair on the other side of the room, and she immediately sat onto it, letting out a soft breath when she curled up and rested her head on the armrest.

I stared at her for too long, hearing her moan gently as she curled up further, and she settled down, getting comfy.

"Tessa," I said then, watching her stiffen, "what are you doing?"

She sat up immediately. "Uh. Nothing! Just... just checking out this armchair. It's nice."

I arched a brow. "Are you stalking me?"

"No…" she said quietly.

"Why were you getting on the armchair?" I questioned. "Were you going to watch me sleep?"

"No…" she said again.

"Are you lying to me?" I demanded. "If you are, I don't take lies well, Tessa."

She was silent for a moment. "I was going to fall asleep on the chair, actually. I wasn't going to watch you."

"Why?" I asked her.

She was silent then.

My lashes immediately lowered. "You just wanted a presence, didn't you? Are you scared?"

She was still quiet.

"Get in with me," I said to her. "Come, now. Sleeping on an armchair for the night doesn't look comfy."

"It's okay," she assured me. "It's quite comfy."

"Tessa," I warned, getting pissed, "I won't ask twice."

She sighed then. "Yes, sir…."

And she got up, stepping over to the bed immediately.

I watched as she crawled under the covers and then gazed up at me, eyes sparkling.

I scanned her form.

She stared at me again.

"Couldn't sleep?" I asked her then.

"Dreaming of you," she responded.

Annoyance filled me. "You liar."

"You look so good shirtless," she told me, a smile spreading across her face, "and you're so cute when you're angry."

I glared then, low growls escaping my mouth. "Are you testing me?"

"Why would I test you?" she questioned. "You don't like being tested."

"I don't appreciate your manipulation, Tessa."

"You don't appreciate anything," she told me.

I sat up then, eyes widening. "Excuse me?"

"You heard what I said."

My glare sharpened. "Continue with this and I won't be kind to you tonight."

She just gazed up. "I don't believe you. You're just a wimp... *sir*."

I shot off the bed, grabbing her by the hair and dragging her out of the bed.

She cried out, collapsing onto the ground when I pulled her up and shoved her face to meet mine.

Her eyes were wide, shaking.

"Do you want to be punished, Tessa?" I questioned her. "Fine, then. Let's go."

And I pulled her up and dragged her out the door, hearing her gasp when she tumbled after me.

After making it across the hall to the sex room, I shoved her in.

She collapsed on the ground, on her hands and knees.

I immediately closed the door, stepping around her as she caught her breath.

And I went to the cabinet, opening the doors and immediately finding my cane and three vibrators.

I took them out and made my way over to her. "On your knees."

She obliged, struggling to get on her knees.

"Strip to your panties," I ordered, pointing the cane threateningly to her.

She listened, pulling off her T-shirt and bra, leaving her only in a pair of bright pink panties.

I immediately snapped the cane against her back.

She cried out, bending forward at the impact.

"Sit up," I snapped.

She listened, sitting up for me.

I then cracked it against her right breast.

She let out a sob, curling in on herself.

I slapped it against her back again, and she cried out, once more. "I said, *sit up*."

She listened, once more.

Immediately, I cracked it against her left breast, and she winced at the action, whimpering.

I then whipped her right breast, then left again, then right again.

I then snapped it against her stomach.

She let out a cry of pain, curling in on herself as she shielded her stomach from more blows.

"I said, SIT UP," I ordered again.

Breathing shakily, she struggled to a seating position.

I stepped around her. "Safe word?"

"Bubbles..." she said then.

"Good girl," I responded. "Now set your hands behind your back and spread your legs. Keep them open or else I'll tie you down."

She listened, propping herself up with her hands before she spread her legs, gazing up at me. "My panties?"

"Nothing can shield you from me," I stated then, glaring down at her. "You're going to be taught a lesson, and you're going to take it."

Her eyes glowed mischievously. "Yes, sir."

I then cracked the cane against her panties, and she gasped, tipping her head back as tears filled her eyes.

I didn't give her a break.

I slapped it against her again, and again, and again, and again, and again.

She was screaming by the twentieth time but listened to me and kept her legs open.

I stopped then.

She collapsed onto her back; her legs still spread as she caught her breath.

I set the cane aside, sighing as I stepped over to my cabinet and set my finger on my chin.

"Hmmm..." I said then, "what to do while punishing you?"

I heard her still gasping for breath behind me.

"Mmmm..." I said then. "I'm going to torture you senseless."

I then pulled out a small anal vibrator and two dildo ones that fit well in her panties, finally ending with a sticky clit stimulator.

After grabbing those, I pulled out more binding rope and tape, making my way back over to her. "Stand up."

"Yes, sir..." she whispered, immediately standing.

"Stand against the wall," I demanded, nodding to a specific one where there were hooks.

She walked over to the wall and gazed up at me.

I just stepped over to her, dropping the toys and just grabbing the rope. "This is going to make a very good picture."

Her brows drew together in confusion.

I just caught her wrists, binding them together and she let me.

Immediately after, I pulled them up until they were high above her head and attached the rope to a pair of cuffs that were on the wall.

I then sighed, grasping her ankles and pulling them apart.

She watched as I cuffed her right and left ankle to the wall, spreading her open for me (with her panties, of course). It didn't stop there, I cuffed her upper arms, stomach, thighs, and calves to the wall.

She was then immobile. The only thing that could leave the wall was her head.

"Mmm," I said then, lightly slapping her right breast as she winced. "Look at you. Such a sexy picture. You'd be a good model."

She just stared down at me nervously.

I then moved and caught the anal vibe, clit stimulator, as well as the vibing dildo, and I leaned down, lightly pulling open her panties to reveal her soft silkiness.

"Look at you," I said then, smirking. "Such a twisted girl. Dripping wet already."

She whimpered as I ran my thumb along her vulva, and then drew back, rubbing my thumb and forefinger together.

I then looked down and smiled, inserting the anal vibrator as she winced, and secondly I inserted the dildo, hearing her moan.

After lightly taping the sticky patch to her clit and stretching out the wire to the batteries, I pulled her lace back over to hide them, tucking in the battery pack on the waistband of her panties.

She looked up at me when I stepped back and smiled, picking up the vibrators and tape, and walked back over to her.

I got to work then, sliding one vibrator into the waistband of her underwear, and pushing it in until it hovered over her clit, and I taped it to her stomach to hold it in place.

Right after, I taped another one to her thigh, directly to the right of the clit to press against the side through the cloth, and I did the same with the left.

I smiled up at her angrily. "Can't have you screaming, can we? You're going to wake the neighbors."

I then pulled open some tape, and her eyes widened when I stuck it over her mouth.

I just locked eyes with her. "Snap three times if you want to stop, remember?"

She nodded.

"Good girl."

After I was satisfied, I walked back over and caught my cane, setting it politely down onto the bed before grasping all the remotes I needed.

I sat onto the bed then, sighing as I propped myself up on the headboard and watched her.

I crossed my legs over the other, eyes darkening.

She just stared at me nervously.

"Let me explain to you what I just did," I said to her then, setting my back against the headboard. "You have a vibrating dildo inside you as well as an anal one that can go up to very high speeds. They're the best of the best. Secondly, you have three vibrators stimulating your clit from all directions, and you cannot move them while writhing. And lastly..." I just watched her, "you have a stimulator taped directly to your clit. An electric one."

Her eyes widened immediately, in horror mixed with amazement.

"It can go up to very overwhelming volts," I said to her, smiling still. "Along with everything else, well... that's going to paint a very pretty picture."

She just stared at me still.

"Now..." I said then, "come however much you want. I don't care. In fact... come as fast as you want. The clit torture will be quite amusing."

She continued staring at me helplessly.

"I'm setting no time limit," I responded then, "I'll keep torturing you until I've had my fill. I hope this teaches you a lesson for provoking me, Tessa."

Her eyes glistened, clearly nervous but excited at the same time.

I picked up a remote, clicking it. "Anal stimulation."

She winced as it started vibrating inside her.

"Pussy stimulation," I clicked another button.

She threw her head back, moaning softly.

"Three clit vibrators," I said then, clicking another button.

She tensed when they started torturing her.

I just watched her for a moment, eyes darkening. "You know what...? I think I just want to get straight to it and set everything to high."

Her eyes widened as she stared down at me.

I just smirked.

And I immediately clicked all remotes to high, hearing her gasping through the tape before I picked up the clit shocking remote.

Her head tipped back, moans escaping her mouth as all the vibrators burrowed inside and outside her filled her with pleasure.

I just smiled. "Here we are. Time for a little pain."

She just looked down at me.

I just kindly turned a dial to low.

She groaned, dropping her head back to the wall as her entire body shook with all the stimulation.

I then turned it to medium.

She started crying softly, her knees bending as she fought to close her legs, but the bindings held her open.

"You're not screaming," I told her, eyes dark. "I want to hear you scream."

And I turned it to high.

And she did.

A loud, muffled screech burned from the tape on her lips as she writhed against the wall, fighting the bindings hardly.

Her hands, knees, and elbows pounded on the plaster, and her head dropped back, continuously hitting the cushion on the wall.

She continued screaming, tears slipping from her eyes as she continued fighting.

Until her eyes rolled to the top of her head, and her body shook violently.

I knew in that moment, that she came.

Poor girl.

I wasn't stopping yet.

Right as it ended, her eyes widened in horror, and I could tell that her clitoris grew a hundred times more sensitive.

She screamed even *louder*, pounding her body against the wall as her body continued to shake violently, and I watched in amusement as she continued the fight the bindings.

I hope she learned her lesson.

I was not to be trifled with.

As she continued screaming in pain and pleasure, I looked up at her hands to find them closed tightly.

She looks so overwhelmed and she's still not using her safe word.

This girl was odd.

I let her writhe, scream, and fight for another ten minutes before I had my fill.

I then shut everything off.

She slumped against the wall then, catching her breath.

I sighed and stepped over to her, ending at her form before I took out all toys and devices, tossing them aside.

I'll clean it up later.

I then untied her.

She collapsed onto me.

I just kept her against me as I picked her up and carried her over to the bed. "I'm not done with you yet. I want to eat you first."

I then tossed her down, and she gasped, bouncing back up when I spread her legs and draped them over my shoulders when I bent down, pulling her panties to the side.

And I leaned forward... and drank.

She gasped, kicking out her legs as the extra sensitivity, but I didn't stop.

She was so wet... all of this was going to go to waste. I couldn't let it go like that. I wanted to feast upon her.

Tessa kept kicking out her legs, fighting me as I kept her wide open, devouring her softness as I suckled onto her and let her thread her fingers through my hair.

I just smiled when she tensed, and the finally she came again.

She cried out this time, back arching when she stretched out her legs, her eyes rolling to the top of her head.

Her body spasms were beautiful... vibrating in my mouth.

I kept drinking until she finished, and I pulled away.

Her legs dropped, and she slumped against the bed, catching her breath.

I immediately got up and pulled the tape from her mouth.

She dropped her head to the side, her eyes dark and weary.

I then lifted her, and she remained limp in my arms when I carried her to the bathroom.

"Are we done...?" she whispered quietly.

"We're done," I promised her.

She just set her head on my shoulder, and I turned on the shower.

"I can't stand..." she told me.

"I know," was my response.

That's why I was carrying her.

When the shower was warm enough, I just quickly pulled off my clothes—somehow while holding her—and stepped into the shower.

Not bothering to set her down, I got to work.

I massaged shampoo into her scalp, spread antiseptic wash into the markings from the cane, and then lastly washed off her pussy, being extra gentle this time.

She didn't react, clearly too tired to.

When I finished washing her, I shut off the shower and carried her out, wrapping her in a towel.

Immediately, knowing she needed rest, I dried her off and then dressed her in my previous T-shirt, letting myself remain shirtless when I carried her back to my bedroom.

Her head was slumped on my chest; she was clearly exhausted beyond words.

I think she's already asleep.

And I laid her in bed, getting in beside her, and covered us in the blankets.

After pulling her to my chest, I closed my eyes, snuggling my face into her neck.

Tessa was still unconscious from last night's rounds, breathing softly against my sheets as her lashes fluttered with her dreams.

I smiled a little, setting my hand under my head as I watched her.

She just remained asleep.

Wanting to see more of her face, I pulled some of her hair away from her cheeks and tucked it behind her ear.

She moaned in annoyance, shifting.

I just watched as she sank back into the sheets and dreamt, once more.

And almost seconds later, her lashes parted.

I smiled down at her. "Hey there, Sweet girl."

She moaned a little and rubbed her eyes, sighing when she set her arms back down onto the bed.

I just watched her gently, brushing some hair away from her eyes. "Do you want your reward now or are you still too sore?"

She just watched me curiously. "I get a reward?"

"Yes," I said gently. "You did well last night."

She then shifted onto her side; eyes dark. "Am I a good girl?"

I watched her now, wondering if she was testing me or not. "Why do you ask?"

She then looked pretty numb, and she stared down at the bed.

"Angel?" My brows drew together.

"I was never a good girl..." she said then, more to herself. "I was always punished."

My eyes suddenly grew dark. "Tess...."

She just set her head on the pillow, and it got me deep in my head—her expression—how she looked incredibly uneasy and unsure of her whereabouts.

I then tucked some hair behind her ear, making her gaze up at me. "He can't hurt you anymore."

I could almost hear her next words:

But you can?

Although her response was different, "Do I get to spend another night with you?"

My smile softened. "Do you like spending the night with me?"

She nodded. "I don't feel alone anymore... He always... kept me in a locked room. And well, Alexis hates me now."

My lips parted and I just ran my thumb along her temple when she looked up at me.

What have I been doing? I'd been punishing her when in reality... she needed more. She needed me to be kind.

I could be kind.

"Why are you looking at me like that...?" she said nervously. "Did I say too much?"

"No, it's alright," I said then, watching her curiously. "Can you get on your back for me?"

"Yeah," she said gently, rolling onto her back. "Are you going to whip me again?"

"No," I responded, pulling open a drawer next to me and pulling out a vibrator. "You don't deserve that. You did nothing wrong."

You deserve to come a thousand times. You deserve pleasure among pleasure.

After all... all you do is listen to me, and I fear that's what he taught you.

Her brows drew together. "Hey, uhm... I can please you after. I can stroke you again... can I?"

"No," I told her lightly lowering my arm under the covers.

It's you who deserves to come right now.

"Did I do something...?" She sounded very nervous.

"Yes," I responded, setting my head on her shoulder as I pressed the vibrator directly to her citrous. "You're too much of a good girl."

And I turned it on.

She winced, tightening the muscles there as she let out a soft moan.

When she struggled, I lightly pulled my ankle against hers, spreading her more as she fought the pleasure.

"Remember what I said?" I asked her. "Bend at the knees, then spread."

She listened, bending at the knees, and the moment she spread, she cried out, arching her back.

"It's alright..." I said gently. "Breathe."

She let out a soft cry, arching her back.

"You're a good girl," I promised her with a smile. "You deserve this, so take it like a good girl, okay?"

She nodded, catching her breath slowly before she let out a long cry.

Immediately, she came.

Her back arched, and she cried out, arching her back as her body shook with her pleasure... and her eyes just rolled to the top of her head.

I took it away before she could experience post orgasm torture.

And her back set against the bed, catching her breath.

I set the vibrator aside and gazed down at her, lightly running my fingers through her hair. "You okay?"

She nodded, keeping her eyes closed.

It was later that night, and Tessa as well as I spent the day apart.

She went to her college class with the bodyguards at her sides, and she came back at around six o'clock.

Since I was busy working on my finances, one of the guards bought her some fast food and she feasted alone.

I felt pretty bad for it, but... I was going to make it worth her while.

It was midnight by the time she made it upstairs, and she opened her door.

The moment her eyes locked on me sitting on her bed with my legs kicked up, her lips parted.

"Uhm..." she said quietly, "are we spending the night again?"

"Mmm—hmm," I responded gently. "I think I'm going to treat you good tonight."

Her brows drew together.

I just stood up and stepped over to her, making her blink when I lightly caught her jacket and lowered it over her arms.

She watched me curiously, clearly wondering what I was doing.

This is how... I thought to myself, *I teach her how to love again.*

She watched me when I helped her out from her skirt, and then lastly her bra without taking her shirt off.

Finishing with taking the clip out from her hair, her long, dark locks spilled down her back, she looked up at me hazily.

I smiled at her, admiring her form.

Her eyes grew dark, and she started taking off her shirt.

"No," I told her, and she stopped. I just watched her seriously. "No."

She watched me again, but then bowed. "Yes, sir."

And she got onto her knees before me, lowering her head.

I just gritted my teeth, not in the mood for this.

But I knelt before her, lightly running my hand over her head when she gazed up hazily.

I just smiled. "Don't submit to me tonight. Just let me treat you nice, okay?" I held out my hand.

She stared down at it for a moment before looking up at me nervously.

"It's okay," I said gently. "I'm not tricking you."

I'd never trick you.

I'm not him.

She then gently set her hand on mine, and I helped her up.

"Lay on the bed for me, okay?" I asked her.

She nodded and laid down, gazing over at me when I walked over and caught some make-up remover wipes.

She closed her eyes when I started scrubbing it off... her eyeliner, her blush, her concealer.

All until her natural beauty showed itself.

Immediately after, I stepped over to her belongings before I found a bottle of some medication.

I glanced back at her when she sat up. "What's this...?"

She looked oddly shy. "Uhm... an antipsychotic. I have it for my Bipolar Disorder."

"Oh."

She has bipolar?

I then scanned the instructions before popping one in my hand, and I caught a glass of water before stopping at her.

I sat beside her at the bed, handing it to her.

"Do you want me to take it…?" she asked me gently. "I'll have a higher sex drive if I don't."

The fucker treated this as a bad drug to her, didn't he? Didn't let her take it so she'd be his slave more willingly without her self-control.

"Take it," I pressed.

She nodded and plopped it in her mouth, swallowing down water seconds later.

I took the cup from her and looked back at her. "Alright, you ready for bed?"

She nodded numbly.

I pulled back the sheets and got under them, setting my back against the headframe when I looked back at her. "Come, come."

She just crawled over to me and knelt by my jeans, starting to undo them.

I set my hand on hers. "Stop."

She gazed up nervously.

I knew very well she felt bad and was trying to get me to be happier.

But this wasn't going to make me feel better. Making *her* feel better was going to make *me* feel better.

"Don't do that," I whispered to her. "Just sit on my lap and cuddle with me, okay?"

"C…cuddle?" she sounded very cautious but very excited at the word.

I smiled. "Do you like the idea of that?"

She nodded. "Yes."

"The come on," I opened my arms.

She let out soft breaths and got onto me, settling sideways in my lap as I wrapped my arms around her.

After pulling the covers over her, she set her head on my chest, getting comfy.

I turned off the lamp on the beside and got her close to me.

"Such a sweet girl…" I whispered. "Go to sleep, okay?"

She snuggled her face into my neck. "Kay."

I smiled down at her.

You'll learn.

You'll learn that I mean you no harm, Angel.

And you'll learn that you're now mine.

You're not his, and you never were.

"And I don't deserve you, but I can't let you go," I whispered, but she was already asleep, breathing against me.

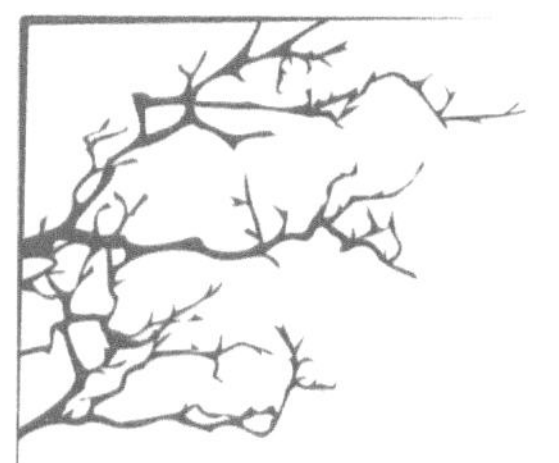

8

Tessa

Present

"When is Miles coming back?" I asked one of the body-guards as he stood by the door to my right.

"He said he'd be back at six, ma'am," was his response.

I hummed in agreement, finishing with cooking the eggs and set them on a plate on my right. "I made some eggs. Maybe you and your friend want some?"

"No, we're alright, ma'am." He kept straight by the door. "We appreciate your kindness, though."

I nodded and stepped over to the counter, starting to prick at my meal before taking a small bite.

But a walkie talky on the man's hip beeped. "Movement found in the east forest," someone said, making the bodyguard look down. "Subject description matching one of Johnathan the killer. Heading for the client's house through the forest in the back! Code 150! *150!*"

The bodyguard suddenly stood up straight and gazed down at me. "Ma'am, we have to go."

My brows drew together as the panic brimmed inside me. "What about Miles?"

"We'll let him know about your whereabouts," he respond-ed, catching my arm and dragging me up. "We need to go!"

He pulled me toward the front door.

The panic inside me deepened.

"Wait!" I cried then. "Miles! We need to call Miles! He'll be targeted if he comes here!"

And I couldn't deal with that. I couldn't lose him.

The guard ignored my attempts at fighting and tossed me into the backseat of his car.

I cried out, tumbling before he got into the driver's seat and immediately started the car, driving off seconds later.

I scrambled to a sitting position, pulling my phone from my pocket.

I then dialed Miles.

It rang once, twice...

"Hello?"

"Miles!" I yelled then, catching my breath. "Don't come back to the house! Please! Don't!"

"Tessa?" he said then, voice dark. "What happened? Did someone come over?"

"They heard him in the forest, and I don't know where they're taking me!" I told him. "Please, don't come back! I'll let you know my location once we arrive!"

Before he could answer, the phoneline clicked, and I gasped for breath, looking down at my phone to find "call disconnected" flashing on the screen.

I then gazed out the window, finding us entering the forest; the dead drop zone.

It was almost an hour drive, and every second consisted of a day itself, and I was nearly sobbing when we found a cabin in the woods, and the driver exited the car, coming to my side seconds later.

He opened my door. "Alright, ma'am. If you'll please follow me—"

A gunshot immediately echoed through the woods, and I screamed.

The bullet sliced right in between the guard's eyes, and he fell forward before crumpling to the ground.

My heart started burning with fear, and I stared up to find a familiar man with dark black locks and hardened eyes lowering his gun.

The large, sadistic smile immediately showed itself, and it reminded me of all those years ago... when he found out I'd been trying to escape.

My eyes widened, breaths stilling.

Johnathan.

How did he find me?!

HOW?!

I immediately scrambled away, gasping when I rounded the car.

"Teresaaaaaa," Johnathan called, making my eyes widen. "Come baaaaaack."

I just shot into the forest, gasping for breath when trees flashed by me at a hundred miles an hour.

And I could hear him following me.

"Why are you running?" he yelled from behind me, laughing as if we were playing a gentle game of chase. "Come, now. Don't you think it's time to give up?"

I kept rushing forward, feeling sticks and branches crack across my face, but could barely register it.

"Teresa!" he sing-songed. "Come baaaaaaaaaack."

Tears spilled down my cheeks, and I urged myself forward, trying hard not to cry.

It wasn't going to fix anything.

"I paid for you," he called from behind me. "I paid for your life, and this is how you repay me? Come, now. If you stop running, I'll be kind and not hurt you."

I just dashed around a tree, shooting to the right and gasping as tears burned down my cheeks.

"Teresa!" he yelled then. "Stop this *instant*!"

Before I could even register the words, another gunshot echoed through the woods.

Something sharp sliced into my calf, and I screamed, tumbling sideways...

Where a cliff rested.

I then cried out, falling down the hill and tumbling among the sharp rocks, going faster the farther I got.

My arms scraped open, my knees, my hands... I could feel the dirt clog the wounds.

Until I tumbled to a stop at the bottom.

I started crying, tears slipping down my cheeks as I remained on my stomach, unable to move.

I was in pain... everything hurt. I was agonized, uneasy, burdened.

The blood stuck onto me, the bullet in my calf pressing against muscle... I couldn't... move.

Distantly, I heard Johnathan sliding down the hill, and I sobbed louder.

He dropped onto his feet right next to me, circling around with that large smile. "I warned you." He then knelt down. "You know I don't like hurting you, Teresa, but you didn't listen. This is what happens when you aren't a good girl."

He then caught me by my hair and dragged me forward.

I screamed as the pain sliced into my scalp, grabbing his wrist as I struggled against his grip.

"Good girls are quiet," he stated then, continuing to drag me forward.

"Please..." I whispered quietly, "I don't want to die."

He dropped me then... at the base of a tree, and I collapsed onto the ground, tears staining my cheeks.

"I'm not going to *kill* you," he said then, tipping his head to the side. "I paid good money for you, why would I want to kill you?"

I just continued sobbing, the pain bursting through me like acid.

"You're mine, Teresa," he said in a dangerous tone. "Understand that. You are mine; you forever will *be* mine, and I'm going to LOCK YOU INSIDE THE DUNGON UNTIL YOU REALIZE IT."

I just remained on the ground, continuing to sob into the dirt.

"Now, it's time to come home," he said as he stepped toward me. "You fight, I shoot your other leg, understand?"

"No..." I whispered as he continued forward, "no! I don't want to go back! Please!"

"Sorry, Honey, but you don't have a choice," he told me then, smirking as he reached down, catching my hair as he shoved my face to his. "Now be a good girl and *be quiet*."

He pulled me up, smile darkening when he was about to turn...

But another gunshot echoed through the woods, and I screamed in horror.

Johnathan froze, remaining still as he stared off into the distance.

I just looked up, breaths stilling when I found him weaving from one foot to the other.

The moment I saw blood slipping down the back of his head... from a hole about an inch wide, I froze.

What...?

And he tumbled forward, collapsing with the dirt, all movements stilling.

I started breathing shallowly, looking around for what happened.

But when I gazed up, I saw Miles standing about fifty feet in front of me, Ace and Kylo behind him as he held up one of his guns that he got from his eighteenth birthday.

I stared in horror.

He just lowered the gun remorselessly, eyes dark. "Motherfucker."

When all of their eyes locked on me, I froze, whimpering.

Ace immediately ran over to me, Kylo behind him.

I felt my breaths shutter as mud and blood stuck to my face, and Ace knelt beside me.

"Are you hurt, Tessa?" he asked me.

I felt my eyes water, breaths stilling.

I was dreaming... right?

But it all felt too real, the pain, the fear... the horror.

Kylo assessed my body before he cursed. "He got her in the leg."

Miles immediately shoved him away. "Back off, ass wipe."

Kylo stood and backed away, throwing his hands up innocently.

I could distantly recall Miles being mad at him for something... but I couldn't remember what it was. Something told me it was related to Alexis... a couple days ago, something he called me.

God, I couldn't think straight.

"Tess," Miles said, looking me in the eyes, but I felt distant, "Tess, can you hear me?"

I just watched my world fade from red to black, framing at the edges.

Miles just looked at Ace. "Call an ambulance."

"On it," he pulled out his phone. "We're out of the dead zone anyway."

Right as he pulled the phone to his ear, Miles looked back at me. "Hey."

I remained silent, breaths shuttering.

He just brushed my hair away from my face, wincing when he saw the scrapes covering me. "You're bleeding all over."

Ace then put down his phone. "They're on the way. There's a fire station a mile up the road."

"Thanks," Miles answered, smiling at me. "Hey, sweet girl. Can you focus your eyes on me?"

I couldn't... I couldn't focus on anything.

"She's distraught," Kylo said from beside us. "I don't think she can hear you."

"Where's Nick?" Ace demanded.

"He got caught up in traffic," Kylo answered. "Should be here soon."

"Well, it's a shame to say he missed the party."

"Tess," Miles said again, running his thumbs under my eyes, "can you hear me?"

I remained silent, breath shuttering.

"Give her a break," Kylo groaned. "She's in shock. How many times do I have to say this?"

Miles immediately gritted his teeth. "I DIDN'T ASK FOR YOUR OPINION. I ALSO DIDN'T ASK YOU TO FUCKING INSULT HER WHEN SHE WAS TRYING TO CALM ALEXIS DOWN!"

Kylo just threw his hands up. "I was just upset, Jesus. All you guys are always so mad at me."

"I wonder why," Ace snapped back, "it's not like you put a tracking device in Aspen's arm so she could be murdered."

"And it's not like you outwardly insult my girlfriend for trying to calm your slut down," Miles shot back.

"*Hey.*" Kylo's tone sharpened. "You call her that again and I fucking shoot you, understand?"

"She is one," Ace shot back. "She's a fucking hooker. You pay for her so much you're growing an attachment to her, fuck-ass."

"Shut it, dickweed," Kylo growled.

I distantly heard sirens in the background.

Miles just looked down at me. "I'm going to pick you up, okay, Angel?"

I remained silent, my vision growing blurry around the edges.

Miles just gently scooped me up, and my body tightened when he started carrying me to a path that went up the cliff and to the road.

"Dead..." I whispered quietly, "he's dead."

Miles just looked down at me.

"He was killed..." I whispered, "the bodyguard."

"John Dickweed is gone, too, Tessa," Kylo said then.

"Shut it, fuckass," Ace snapped.

"If you keep calling me that, Imma sock your dick," Kylo shot back.

But we made it to the road, and Miles kept me in his arms... his muscles so strong they held me perfectly.

Almost five seconds later, the ambulance rolled to a stop ahead of us, and they came rushing out with a stretcher.

"Sir, if you could please set her down," one of the workers said.

Miles gently lowered me onto the stretcher, and I felt tears burning down my cheeks when he pulled the blanket over me and ran his thumb along my forehead. "You'll be okay..." he promised me.

"He's gone now."

I gazed up at Miles when he carried me gently back into his house, eyes glistening with his reflection when we entered the second floor and to his bathroom.

We had gotten out of the ER a couple hours ago—they got the bullet out of me and said other than the wound, I just had a lot of scrapes, nothing broken—and Miles took me home... Well... to *his* home.

"Alright," he said to me, setting me on the toilet, "let's give you a nice shower, and when Ace and the others get here, I'll have them bring up your crutches, okay?"

I nodded. "Kay."

He smiled down at me and turned on the shower, going to get some soaps before making his way back over to me.

Afterward, he helped me strip, getting my skirt and shorts off... and then finally my undergarments.

After stripping himself, he picked me up again and carried me into the shower.

I winced when the warm water rained down onto me, and my eyes glistened when I watched him.

He held one arm under my bottom, holding me like a child... and he was strong enough to.

It only took two seconds before he started washing me.

I smiled, setting my head on his shoulder when he scrubbed my arms and legs, being extra gentle with my scrapes, and avoiding the wound on my leg directly.

I parted my lashes and stared down at his chest, feeling my heart flutter when he started massaging the shampoo into my scalp.

I sniffled and kept my head on his chest, loving how warm he was.

When he rinsed me off, I kept my eyes on his pectorals, desperately wanting to play with them.

"You okay, baby?" he asked me.

"Yeah," was my response. "Just... comfy."

He smiled and started running conditioner through my strands. "That's good. I live to make you comfortable."

I sniffled and closed my eyes, loving how I was pressing to him.

"Sir...?" I said quietly.

"Miles, baby. Miles."

"Oh, yes, right," I said then. "Are you... alright?"

He was silent then, now gently rubbing my back to soothe me. "I'm just... glad you're okay is all."

"Are you mad?" I wondered.

"Not at you," he responded. "At everything else, though."

I was silent.

"Everyone's so cruel to you, Tessa," he said to me, scrubbing my hair again. "I won't stand for it anymore. I almost..." he was silent for a moment, "I almost lost you, and I haven't even gotten to show you how good of a boyfriend I can really be."

I stared down at him gently.

Boyfriend...? He liked me that way?

I thought I was just another one of his submissives... and that once he was done with me, I'd be on my own again.

I just gently set my hand on his chest, trying to lighten the mood. "Can I touch? It looks so bouncy."

"Go ahead," he said to me, chuckling.

I started playing with his pecs then, running my hand on the smooth skin as he continued scrubbing me senseless.

After a moment of touching him, I set my head on his chest. "Miles...?"

"Yes, Sweets?"

"Can I..." I hesitated.

"Can you, what?" he pressed. "Finish your sentences, baby."

I pushed it out then. "Can I stay... with you?"

He was silent for a moment, and I felt the cold develop inside me at his hesitation.

But he finally spoke, "You can stay with me forever."

I looked up, shocked.

He just smiled, running his thumb along the widow's peak on my forehead. "Only if you sleep in my room, though, okay? I want to see your face when I wake up every morning. I've been longing it since high school."

I felt my eyes start glistening with his words, and my heart fluttered. "So I'm not just... another one of your toys?"

"I'm *your* toy," he responded with a smile. "Not the other way around. Play with me however you like, pretty girl. And don't break me," his eyes softened, "that's all I ask."

My lips parted, and I felt warmth bleed into my veins. "Do you like me?"

"I *love* you," he corrected, eyes dark. "And I didn't realize just how much I did until I almost lost you." His voice grew thin. "I'm sorry, Angel. I'm very sorry that I left you so long ago. You didn't deserve that."

I just watched him with a level of kindness I never thought I could have. "You love me?"

He smiled then, clearly seeing my hidden excitement. "Yes."

I then looked down at his chest and set my head on his collarbone, and he ran his fingers through my hair.

Twenty minutes later, Miles carried me downstairs in one of his freshly clean T-shirts and my shorts.

He also changed my bandages after the shower.

"Hey, dude," Nick said then, standing up before pausing. "Oh, you're carrying the girl. I guess no handshakes for me. Sniff, sniff."

"Oh, shut it," Ace's wife, Aspen said, laughing. "You're such a child."

Ace just pulled her back onto his lap, and she smiled over at him when he wrapped an arm around her. "I never told you to get up."

"Well, I'm *sorry*, your majesty."

"How are you feeling?" Alexis said then, making my eyes shoot over to find her standing in a corner, right next to Kylo who was vaping.

I never responded, just looked back down at Miles's chest as the cold consumed me again.

I heard Alexis shift, clearly uncomfortable.

"Kylo," Miles said then, tone sharp, "do me a favor and stop vaping in the house. And go get her crutches from my car."

He just growled, giving Miles the middle finger before stepping back out the front door.

Alexis remained in the corner, watching us. "Tess..." she said then, voice dark, "I'm sorry. I treated your horribly. I said such cold things to you when all you were was just scared."

I continued staring down at Miles's chest, feeling the air thicken with my exhaustion and numbness.

"Tess," she urged, "Tess, I'm so sorry."

"It's alright," I whispered then, "it's my fault."

Everyone then looked to me, surprised.

"I should've never gotten into your lives with him on the loose. I just thought he was gone for good... but he wasn't. I'm sorry that I hurt you, Lexie."

Miles suddenly slapped my ass, and I cried out.

"Ow!" I said then, looking up at him. "What the hell?!"

His eyes were dark, angry. "Stop it."

I just thinned my lips. "Stop what?"

"Don't say things like that," he responded in a dark tone. "Did you seriously expect yourself to deal with it alone? How can you be so cruel to yourself, Tessa?"

"I'm glad you told me," Alexis said then, making all of us look over at her. "Or else... you would've been dealing with this for the rest of your life. Alone. No one to talk to."

Lexie gazed up. "He never hurt me, he hurt you. Remember that. I was being a bitch for yelling at you, I'm sorry."

My eyes darkened, and I stared back at Miles's chest. "Thanks."

It's nice to know that we were still friends.

She shrank back against the wall, fixing her jeans.

The front door opened then, and Kylo carried my crutches in, slamming the door shut and setting them on the couch seconds later.

"Alright, Kylo, make dinner," Nick said.

"What?!" he snapped. "Why me?!"

"Because you make the best food and you were the one who hurt her the most," Ace responded then. "Go make the dinna."

He just growled and stormed into the kitchen. "I'm spitting in all your meals."

Everyone just started laughing.

"Hey, Nick," Aspen said then. "Don't you have a girl-friend?"

"Kinda," he responded. "She's just a fling, really."

"Why didn't you bring her?" Ace said.

"She's at her parents' house," he responded, sighing as he leaned back. "They don't like me."

They all emersed in conversation then, and started laughing at some jokes, but I stayed in Miles's arms when he carried me over to the couch and held me in his lap.

"Hey..." Miles said then, voice quiet. "Uhm, Tessa."

"Yeah?" I said, playing with his shirt.

"Remember when you told me, the only thing you didn't want, was to be called Teresa?"

I nodded, setting my head on his collarbone.

"Was it because... *he* called you that?"

"Yes," I said honestly, picking at a loose string.

Miles just ran his fingers through my hair. "Then it's final... I call you Tess or Tessa. Anyone who dares to speak your name as Teresa will hear from me."

I giggled and snuggled my face into his neck, and I could feel him smiling.

"Where's your dad?" he asked me then. "I want to have a word from him."

"Don't worry," I said then, "he's dead."

Miles looked down at me, brows drawing together. "What?"

"He murdered my mother," I said, looking up at Miles gently. "And then sold me off. Both are illegal. He was sentenced for twenty years but one of his inmates killed him."

Miles's lips shaped into an "O".

"Are you glad he's gone?" Miles asked me.

"Yes," I responded, playing with his shirt again. "Very glad."

He just set his cheek on my head, rubbing my back now. "If you get tired, feel free to close your eyes, okay? You're on very strong pain meds."

I nodded.

I watched Miles curiously as he slept on his king mattress in front of me, his eyes fluttering a little as he dreamt.

I held my hands under my head, knowing that he was stark naked under the sheets... it was how he slept... but I couldn't help but stare at his blissful state, wondering how a man could be so beautiful.

I was only in a sports bra and panties, mainly because I was too tired to take them off, but eventually I woke up and couldn't sleep much longer.

And now I was staring at him... and I knew it was creepy, but I didn't care.

After a moment longer, he let out a soft yawn and stretched, immediately opening his eyes to look at me. "You're burning holes into my forehead, Sweetheart."

"Sorry," I said then, smiling, "I can't help it."

He just smiled back, brushing some hair away from my forehead. "Do you need more pain meds?"

"No," I responded gently. "You're just so mesmerizing."

He sighed and set his hand down. "You look a little troubled."

My eyes flicked around his face for a moment. "Why won't you let me please you? Every time I ask... you deny."

"Because I want you to be pleased first," he told me with a smile. "That's why."

"But what about you?"

"I'm fine just the way I am."

I stared at him for too long.

He chuckled. "You're looking at me as if I'd grown two heads."

"Miles..." I whispered gently, "I want you. And I mean I really, really, really want *you*. I don't want a toy."

He pulled some hair away from my lashes. "You really, really, *really*?"

I nodded. "Can I, please?"

"You're hurt, sweetheart."

"I can be gentle."

He just sighed, smiling. "They're sleeping."

"I can be quiet."

He looked at me fully then. "Don't you want to wait until later?"

My eyes flickered to dark again, and I felt my face dull in sadness. "Am I bad girl? Is that why you're denying me? Can't you punish me then?"

"You're not a bad girl," he responded gently. "You've been a very good girl and you've been listening very well. I just don't want to hurt you."

I hesitated then. "Can I lead, then...?"

His eyes softened. "Tessa."

"You can pull your belt around my neck," I told him, smiling. "You can control me."

His smile turned slightly amused. "You want me that bad, huh?"

I nodded.

He sighed, rolling onto his back. "Alright, come on."

My eyes glistened. "Really?"

"Yes," he said, glancing at me, "now, hurry up."

I sat up, wincing slightly as I crawled over to him, and I scrambled off my panties before I straddled him.

"Does that hurt?" he asked me, eyes dark. "We can switch positions."

"No, it doesn't." I knew very well he was talking about the gunshot wound, and I wasn't lying.

I lowered myself a little.

I can already feel him under me.

Oh... he was already rock hard.

Before I could sink down, he caught my hips.

I looked up, confused.

He just smiled. "Hold on."

And he unclipped my bra, lowering it off my arms and tossing it across the room.

And he opened his nightstand drawer, pulling out a large, leather belt as my eyes sparkled.

He fit it kindly around my neck, tightening it just *slightly* so it pressed against my airpipe, and he gripped the end, his other hand on my hip.

Heat flooded down to my favorite spot then, and I looked up at him, waiting for a command.

"Start," he told me, knowing I needed a gentle reminder. "Lower yourself, and then roll your hips on me. Can you do that?"

I nodded.

"Okay," he said then, brow arching, "go too fast and I tighten your collar. You won't like that."

I smiled, aroused. "Yes, sir."

And I lowered my hips, feeling him press inside me.

I whimpered, throwing my head back as the pleasure burned through me.

He tightened the collar, making me gasp. "Start rolling, don't tease me."

I smiled again. "Yes, sir."

And I pulled my hips back and forth, holding my hands on his chest as he groaned, watching me with lust-filled eyes as I kept whimpering.

He set his hand on my hip to control my pace. "Slow down. You're not coming yet, understand?"

I kept the smile, slowing. "Yes, sir."

As I rolled my hips back and forth on him, I relished the feeling of him inside me... how hot he was... how thick he was.

He was so big... this felt so much nicer then in my mouth.

"You're a good listener," his breath was short, catching after every thrust. "I don't think you realize how good of a girl you are."

I just looked up at him. "Then teach me."

His smile darkened, and he pulled the belt, tightening it around my neck. "Go faster."

I rolled onto him, closing my eyes tightly as I steadied myself on his chest.

My hips moved faster than I ever thought they could, and I felt sweat sliding down my temples as I kept going and going.

"Can I...?" I begged him. "Can I, please?"

I tightened, whimpering.

"You can come now," he promised me.

And I let go, crying out as I dropped onto his chest, hearing him groan when I pulled my hips back and forth repeatedly.

My eyes rolled to the top of my head, and I felt the orgasm rattle through me like gold when I clutched onto him desperately.

I could hear him groaning, too.

"Fuck," he growled, holding onto me tightly. "Fuck!"

After I rode both our orgasms out, I weakened onto him, holding my face in his chest as his hands tightened at my back.

Miles reconciled himself first and pulled the blankets over both of us. "Stay there. You're so warm inside."

I smiled. "Weirdo."

He then pulled the belt off me and tossed it across the room, running his fingers through my hair. "Sleep now."

I smiled, burying my face into his neck. "Yes, sir."

And he started rubbing my back, breaths soft. "God... I hadn't felt that good in a long time. I know that saying now... fucking someone you're in love with really does feel different."

I just held my face in his neck, comfy. "I missed you."

"I missed you, too, Angel."

I then decided to say softly. "I love you."

He pulled the covers higher over us, rubbing my back as he lightly kissed my ear. "I love you, too. My beautiful angel."

*T*he end?

Don't miss out!

Visit the website below and you can sign up to receive emails whenever Aspen Wolff publishes a new book. There's no charge and no obligation.

https://books2read.com/r/B-A-NWFAD-EPKLF

BOOKS 2 READ

Connecting independent readers to independent writers.

Did you love *Teach Me How To Love Again*? Then you should read *Catch Me if You Can*[1] by Aspen Wolff and Arianna Courson!

[2]

ASPEN CAMPBELL

I ran from my past; I ran from him because I couldn't bear the anger in his expression any further.

Two years ago, my best friend was murdered by someone I knew, and my entire group of friends demanded to know where that person was.

I couldn't tell them, though. I couldn't. It would put me and her in danger, so I ran.

---

1. https://books2read.com/u/bwkezO

2. https://books2read.com/u/bwkezO

But there was something tugging my mind for those two years, something big, and bad, and dangerous that kept forcing my hands under the sheets when I pictured him.

And then when I realized that I was moving to the same college as him, and I knew I couldn't run forever.

I wanted to protect my sister, but at the same time, his eyes were haunting me.

I wanted him, I needed him, and I didn't know how to ease that pain burning inside me.

Well... I knew how... I just couldn't find a way around it.

ACE CARTER

Oh, I missed her. Oh, how I wanted her to pay for what she did.

She was in my nightmares, and she was in my dreams. I wanted her, I wanted her for years, but that didn't change what she did.

We moved into the same college, and her dorm room was just two floors down from my penthouse, and I couldn't wait for her to move in.

I didn't know how I could resist her then.

We called ourselves a fling back then, but now? Oh, now it was much more. Powerful and dangerous.

Who can resist this game?

It's my move, Aspen Campbell, and I intend to win.

Also by Aspen Wolff

Catch Me if You Can
Obsession
Teach Me How To Love Again

About the Author

Aspen Wolff is an adult romance author who lives in Colorado. She enjoys living with her four dogs and three cats, and also enjoys listening to music endlessly for hours. Her favorite hobbies are writing, drawing, and watching anime. In the future, her dream is to be a famous author for years to come.

www.ingramcontent.com/pod-product-compliance
Lightning Source LLC
Chambersburg PA
CBHW051218160726
47994CB00002B/657